Her Whole Self

Hope you are blessed by the journey...

Her Whole Self

a novella

tracy wainwright

TLC Wainwright Publishing, LLC
VIRGINIA

Her Whole Self

Copyright © 2013 by Tracy L. Wainwright
        Published by TLC Wainwright Publishing, LLC
        P.O. Box 1001
        Toano, VA 23168

All rights reserved. No part of this book may be reproduced, scanned, or distributed in any printed form or by any electronic or mechanical means, including information storage or retrieval systems, without permission in writing from the publisher, except by a reviewer who may quote brief passages in a review.

Scriptures taken from the HOLY BIBLE: NEW INTERNATIONAL VERSION®. Copyright © 1973, 1978, 1984 by International Bible Society. Used by permission of Zondervan Bible Publishers.

Book design by Daniela Bergman, Dear Violet Boutique Photography
www.dearvioletboutique.com
First Printing: 2013

ISBN-10: 0989948501
ISBN-13: 978-0-9899485-0-0

This book is dedicated to my husband, Gary. Words could never express my gratitude for putting up with leftovers for dinner, clutter throughout the house, and extra dust lying around on all the days I got lost in the computer. Thank you for loving my heart from broken to whole. I love you more today than I did yesterday and not as much as I will tomorrow.

To the Lord God Almighty, whom deserves all praise, I cannot believe You've taken a girl who hated writing research papers and turned her into an author. Thank You for all the lessons You've taught me along the way, including that Your timing is always perfect and Your plans are so much better than anything I could have come up with on my own. May You be glorified in everything I do and every word I write.

CHAPTER ONE

Jen gaped at the ring in her palm.

"You can keep it." Ian's voice interrupted her spinning thoughts, questions.

Her gaze flew to his face, meeting his deep, brown eyes. How could he do this? How could he sit beside her on the sofa they'd picked out together calm as a lion after eating his fill of prey?

He'd promised her love, security, and a lifetime together. Instead of fulfilling his pledge of caring for and protecting her heart, he'd smashed it, broken it in tiny bits, and handed it back to her.

Why? Had he ever loved her? Or had it all been a lie?

She swallowed the desire to scream, yell. To scratch the glazed-over, glassy look in his eyes with the oval shaped diamond she'd wrenched off her finger. Something. Anything other than falling to her knees in front of him and begging.

Clever, piercing words. That's what he deserved and what Jen's head raced to find. Her heart, however, won the battle. "Please…don't do this."

Tears streaked down her face and soaked into her jeans.

He furrowed his brow and pulled his lips taunt.

Was he sad? Did he have any feelings towards her? Or was he waiting for her to give up and leave? Either way, he gave no reply.

She held out her hand. It shook almost as much as her voice. "I don't want it."

He narrowed his eyes. "What would I do with it?"

She curled her fingers around the now offending object. Weeks before she'd joyfully shown it off, constantly turning her hand to catch the light in the diamond of promise.

Promise. Hmph.

A sob burst forth despite Jen's effort to swallow it back down.

He stared at the coffee table, glanced at the blank television, looked everywhere, anywhere except her way. He showed no pity, no emotion, no remorse.

He couldn't care less.

She pushed herself up on wobbly legs, hesitating, digging her nails into her palm, feeling the ring once again as it made an indention on her palm. *You coward. Goat. Jerk.* The words stuck in her throat. Only additional, humiliating whimpers escaped as she turned and fled.

At her car, Jen tried to unlock the door four times before the key finally slid into its home. She collapsed on the seat and closed herself in. Alone. Utterly, miserably alone.

She'd given him everything. Her dreams, her desires, her future, her body. And he discarded it all like yesterday's newspaper. Fresh tears raced down her cheeks.

Who was she without Ian? The rearview mirror gave no answers, even when she twisted it for a fuller view. It only showed what she already knew – heartbreak, framed by wavy, dark hair matching the streaks of mascara trailing down her face.

Jen flipped the mirror back into place, punched open her glove box, and threw in the diamond. With a ragged sigh, she slammed the compartment closed. What now? What did she have left?

She leaned back on the headrest. Her job, even if it wasn't a great one. Her apartment, which she barely squeaked by paying her half of the rent on. But at least she shared it with her best friend. And her cat, Peaches, her most faithful companion for the last eight years.

She wiped the most recent tear escapees and cranked the ignition. She'd go home. At least she hadn't lost everything, just almost everything.

I will never leave you.

The words volleyed in her mind. They were familiar, yet foreign; like she'd discovered a postcard from a trip she didn't remember taking. She shook her head and drove home.

As she pulled into her parking space at her apartment twenty minutes later, the words still bounced around like a racquetball in a gravity-free court. The cross dangling from her rearview mirror caught her eye.

Oh. God. Those were His words. Ones she'd learned in a church club years ago. It'd been so long since she'd given Him any thought. For the last two and a half years her thoughts had been consumed by that other him. Ian.

Was God still there? Did He care?

She squeezed her eyes shut. Why would He? And if He did, why would He allow her heart to be ground into mulch?

She opened her eyes and fixed her gaze on the cross. Those five words reverberating again and again: I will never leave you. I will never leave you. I will never leave you.

Why had she left that charm up there all this time? Because she loved her aunt. But now, it reminded her of broken promises and useless fairytales. She yanked it off the mirror and tossed it in the glove box, adding it to her growing collection of meaningless jewelry.

CHAPTER TWO

Silence greeted Jen after she slammed the apartment door. Pam should be there. She tossed her keys and purse on the table by the door. Carrying the pulverized pieces of her heart, she walked across the cozy, if small, den. Peaches darted out of her room, rubbed against her leg and meowed.

Stooping down, she scooped up her beloved feline and nuzzled her against her cheek. "At least *you* won't leave me."

She fell onto the sofa and leaned back, propping her feet on the white-stained coffee table. She reached over and clicked on a lamp. And that's when she noticed them. Boxes. Piled on the dining room table. Stacked in the corner by the front door.

Boxes? "What in the world?"

Peaches gave her the only reply she could. "Meow." Sensing her owner's distress, the cat nudged her hand to garner more attention.

Scooped up again, Peaches traveled down the hallway held gently, but tightly.

The door to Pam's room was closed, but light escaped through the almost inch tall gap at the bottom of the door. Another bad sign. Jen's roommate never stayed up past ten, much less one a.m. What had happened in the forty-eight hours since the friends had shared a Chinese dinner and caught up with each other?

Jen knocked.

The familiar dark eyes haloed by blonde, cropped hair met her gaze. Red lines invaded the normally crystal clear orbs. Mascara-highlighted tear trails traveled down Pam's cheeks, probably matching her own.

Is this the night of broken hearts? "Honey, what's wrong? What's going on? What's with all the boxes?"

"I have to…go." The dark eyes filled as pools. "My-" she hiccupped. "My dad had a stroke yesterday. My mom-" Another hiccup. "Can't take care of him by herself."

Pam turned to her almost empty room, scanning for any stray items to be gathered and rescued.

"But you can't go." Jen's throat tightened. Could her

heart really hurt worse? Bile threatened to push its way up.

Those dark, spilling eyes met hers. Fear. Sorrow. Pain.

"I don't want you to go." She threw her arms around the friend who had supported her. Encouraged her. Fixed her soup when she was sick.

Pam grieved on her shoulder, dampening her sleeve as Jen had earlier soaked her own lap. The friends pulled apart and Jen studied her roommate and confidant.

I'm not the only one hurting.

"I don't want to leave." Pam wiped away her tears with a bulky sweater sleeve. "But how can I not? How could I tell my mom she's on her own? And how can I help her from three states away?"

Jen inhaled the stench of a world changing and breathed it out again. *I can't even tell her. I can't tell my best friend that my heart's been crushed. O, God, why? Two in one night? I thought we were never supposed to fall at the same time.*

Another deep breath of stale, hard air. It escaped through tight lips. "I know. You need to be with your family. Let me help you."

Four hands, two hearts, lives changing, worked side by side. Pam had apparently taken off work and gotten the bulk of her things boxed up. Only a few items remained to go in one half-filled box in the middle of the floor.

Jen picked the book up from the table and ran her hands across the leather cover. How long since her hands had touched her own Bible? She flipped pages and let her eyes roam the open pages briefly.

I will never leave you nor forsake you.

Is that where those words came from? Everyone was leaving her. If God hadn't, why was He letting everyone else?

She closed the book and slipped it into a box.

"Jen?"

She looked up.

"I'm really gonna miss you."

She placed a picture frame in the open box. "I can't even begin to tell you how much I'm going to miss you."

Pam sat on the edge of the bed and shivered. "I never wanted to go back to northern Indiana. Do you know how many inches of snow they've had this year?"

"Twenty?"

"Try fifty-eight." She slid to the floor.

Jen sat next to her friend and leaned against the bed. "Whoa."

"I know. I love the way it snows here in eastern Virginia. A couple inches, a day off, then everything melts and gets back to normal."

A smile broke through and Jen laughed. "It's true.

I can remember only a handful of times we've had snow last more than a couple days. I always loved it though and envied people like you who grew up with feet and feet of it. I think I only saw snow half a dozen times in Alabama. And it was usually just flurries."

"Ugh. It gets old fast."

"I can understand that now."

Silence infiltrated the room as the friends sat shoulder to shoulder. Pam broke it first. "You gonna be okay? I know money's tight with your school loans and everything."

"I'll be alright." Jen refused to compound Pam's worries with the truth.

"I'll be praying for you. I'm so sorry to leave you in such a tight situation."

Jen didn't need prayers. She needed something in her life to stay the same. Normal. Her only response was to lean her head against her best friend's. What would tomorrow bring?

CHAPTER THREE

Jen scooched down further in the over worn sofa cushions, caressed the warm cup of cocoa, and studied the apartment. Technically, it wasn't any emptier than it had been the day before. Only one recliner was missing. The rest of the furniture remained. The room down the hall, however, held nothing. No bed. No dresser. No pictures of friends laughing. No computer or MP3 speakers or beads encasing the window. Everything that gave the room personality, everything that made the apartment theirs, had been packed up, labeled, and moved out.

Along with her best friend.

First, the love of her life abandoned her. Then her bff. Both gone in less than twenty-four hours.

Her tear-stained cheeks had finally dried, but now her head throbbed, refusing to be abated with a single dose of ibuprofen.

Balancing the mug in one hand, she used the other to wrap the blanket tighter around her shoulders. The heaviness she felt didn't come from the afghan. It didn't even all come from the losses she'd dealt with in last few days. One more thing had heaped bricks upon her shoulders: That empty room down the short hall meant more than a lost roommate. It meant the loss of half the rent.

She sipped the cooling liquid. Jen couldn't bring herself to ask Pam for the money. How exactly would that conversation go? "Sorry about your dad's stroke and you having to quit your job and move home, but could you give me a couple months rent?"

No. She couldn't. She wouldn't.

Jen set her mug to the side, sank lower, and buried her head into the soft material gathered in her hands. Leaning forward, she rested her forehead against her knees. *How much can I take?*

Purring answered her question. Peeking out of her cocoon, Jen saw that Peaches had joined her. She scooped up the orange cat and held her close.

"What are we going to do, Peaches? How do we find a roommate in two weeks?" A sigh escaped. Everything had been going so well. She was making it. Doing things on her own. Proved her parents wrong. She was capable, independent, and didn't need anyone.

She didn't *need* a boyfriend, but enjoyed having one. She had looked forward to being married. It was part of the plan.

Her eyes darted to the wedding organizer still lying on the coffee table. Plans. Details decided upon. Meals and colors picked out. Flowers ordered. Songs listed. Dresses tried on. All going up in smoke. She hadn't gotten far enough to think about cancelling everything. Hadn't made a single phone call. The words fell flat and got scrambled every time she thought through the explanations she'd have to make

Maybe I can get some deposits back. Maybe that will pay the rent. For a month anyway. Then what?

Then I'll think of something else. I always do.

The heaviness settled in her heart. What if she didn't come up with something? What if she couldn't find a new roommate? What if she got no deposit money back?

There was always the ring. She could sell it.

Her stomach knotted. Could she really? It seemed so final to even think about getting rid of it.

Peaches leapt from her lap and crossed the room. She stretched, jumped onto a small table and curled up next to the dusty Bible decorating it. The Bible had been a housewarming gift from Jen's aunt when she moved into the apartment. She'd left it out, thinking one day she might find time to read it.

She unfolded her limbs and tossed the blanket aside. The orange ball of fur purred as she brushed her out of the way and picked up the Bible.

I know You said You'd never leave me. But what I need now are answers. Practical, real, tangible answers. I need a wedding canceled and a roommate replaced. I don't need ancient stories and fluffy words.

She wiped the dust off with her sleeve and set the book back on the table. She rubbed Peaches' ear. "I can't sit around and wallow in self-pity any more. That won't get things done." She sighed. "And there's so much to do."

Crossing the room to the kitchen, Jen grabbed a pen and pad of paper. She'd start with a list.

I'll get things done one by one and everything will be okay.

CHAPTER FOUR

Her life on hold for a list. Almost a week after creating it and Jen had only marked a few things off. She thumbed the empty ring finger on her left hand. She could tell herself she didn't need a man in her life. Didn't need to get married, but the truth was she still loved Ian. And her heart ached. She fought the tears. She'd shed enough and would not give into them again.

Peaches purred on the sofa behind her. She stared at the inventory of things left to do. Number one: "Find a Roommate." If only she had more control over it. She'd posted on Facebook, placed an ad in the paper, and asked just about everyone she knew. Not a single bite. She could hang on for two months, maybe.

She wasn't ready to give up, but she really didn't have much of a choice. Her rent, student loan payment, electricity, cell, water, cable, and internet bills relentlessly reminded her so.

What else could she do to find a replacement for Pam? No. Not a replacement. No one could stand in for her best friend. But they could certainly replace her half of the rent.

She could post again. She grabbed her laptop and logged in. A quick browse of status updates and shared videos and she'd send out her plea one more time. She scrolled down the screen for a while then clicked on notifications. One comment on a post.

Her heart sped up. Maybe someone had answered, inquiring about moving in with her. One more tap of the mouse doused her hopes.

She read the comment. "Any luck?"

No! She wanted to scream. *And don't comment unless it's something helpful.*

Jen typed in the local newspaper's name in the search bar and navigated to the classified page. She entered her information. On the final page, the one to enter payment, she paused. More money out for no guarantee of success? She shook her head and closed the browser.

Maybe Leonard's List. At least that was free. She reopened the window, completed the form, and laid her head.

back

What else could she do?

She could call her parents. A shudder travelled up her spine. Not an option. She was not desperate enough to make *that* sacrifice.

Jen moved to number two on her list. "Go out more." She groaned. Sitting around an empty apartment sulking hadn't done her any good. But how was she supposed to go out *and* save every penny of her salary needed to make next month's rent? She'd already sold her engagement ring and cut her grocery bill in half by surviving on sandwiches, noodles, and eggs. A week of eating like that and she felt like she was back in college.

Once again, she traveled to her world of friends via the web. Six hundred and three "friends" and she hadn't had one call to go out since Ian dumped her and Pam moved out. She browsed the event suggestions. Dinner out, bar hopping, and clubbing would cost her money. Besides, she might have to eat like she did while in school, but had no desire to hit the college scene every weekend.

Jen moved the list and her laptop aside and shuffled to the kitchen for a glass of water. She sipped the cold, refreshing liquid as new posts appeared. Watching the updates, she wished she had something to add. Her brain stalled. So far in the last week she'd changed her relationship status and begged for a new roommate. She certainly wasn't going to follow those up with a, "Hey, anyone got anything going on tonight?" Nor did she want to 'share her thoughts.' The world didn't want to know what was on her mind right now.

Clicking on a few of the links, Jen found herself distracted by funny videos and rolling her eyes at ridiculous pictures. Then a new post caught her eye. Marla, a girl she knew in college. "Bored tonight? Strapped for cash? Come hang out with me to watch a totally-free and awesome movie. Refreshments provided. Starts at 7. Corinth Church."

She reread the post. It almost seemed written specifically for her. Hadn't she just been saying she needed to get out of the house but had no money?

But a church movie? Surely that'd be dorky and bore the waves right out of her hair.

Was sitting at home alone any better? Besides, Marla was sweet. They'd studied together a few times for exams. Marla had even invited her to church, but there always seemed to be something better to do. Like hang with her boyfriend.

That worked out well.

Jen hadn't seen her in couple a years. Only once since

graduation, when they ran into each other at a restaurant in Poquoson.

She read the post again and checked the clock. A handful of minutes past six. That gave her plenty of time to get ready and to the church she'd seen the sign for every day on her way to and from work for the last three years. She checked the chat column, but Marla's name didn't show up. She scanned her contacts in her phone. What were the chances Marla's number was still the same? She dialed.

"Hello?"

"Hey, um, Marla, it's Jen. From CNU. I, uh, saw your post about the movie at your church tonight."

"Yes! I'm getting ready now."

"I didn't have any other plans and wondered if I could go with you."

"That'd be great. Want me to pick you up?"

What had she gotten herself into? "No, that's okay. I'll meet you there." *In case I need an escape or something better comes up in the next half hour.*

"Okay. I'll be there about quarter to seven. Do you need directions?"

"No, I'm pretty sure I know where it is"
"Oh, good. Take the exit off the interstate for J Clyde and it's the first road on your left."

Jen mumbled her gratitude and hit end. Had she lost her mind? She x'd out the internet window and closed her laptop. *Guess I need to get a shower.* Her stomach flopped as she shuffled down the hall.

Fifteen minutes later, she stared at her closet. What did one wear to a movie night at church? Surely not a dress. She didn't own many dresses and doubted most would pass religious scrutiny.

Surely jeans and a sweater would work. She snatched the pairing off their respective hangers and slipped them on. After pulling her hair back in a loose braid and applying her make-up, she opened her computer again. A quick scan provided no viable alternatives. Guess she was stuck following through on her word. She'd meet Marla at church, of all places, to watch a movie.

She stroked Peaches, who'd leapt onto her lap and stared at her curiously. "I know. You need a little alone time. I'll get out of your way for a while."

Jen brushed her face against the soft fur and set the feline on the floor. "Let's just hope no one realizes I have no business being in a church."

CHAPTER FIVE

Jen steered her ten-year-old Sentra into the church parking lot and raised her eyebrows at the number of cars filling the spaces. This many people had nothing better to do on a Friday night? Scanning the parking lot, Jen spotted a couple walking beneath the lamp posts toward the back building, arms looped around each other. She groaned.

This was a mistake. She shouldn't have come. Swallowing down the lump suddenly clogging her throat, Jen considered texting Marla that something had come up. Her thumb paused mid-tap as a dark-haired guy brushed past the couple and playfully thumped the male half of the couple on the head.

She watched the playful response and the ensuing banter between obvious friends. The guy who'd broken the romantic stroll laughed easily, making his tanned face more handsome in the surprisingly bright lamp light. He stood quite a bit taller than the couple, who were about equal in height. She couldn't tell anything else about his stature from this distance, especially considering the bulky tan coat he wore.

Jen sat back in surprise. Was she really checking a guy out? Not that she had time for romance with all the other drama occupying her life. Nor did she relish the idea of handing over her pulverized heart to another guy. She hadn't even finished making all the wedding cancellation phone calls. Maybe once all the dust settled she'd consider dating again.

She jumped at the tapping on her window. She glanced left meeting Marla's flushed, smiling face. *Guess I have to go in now.*

Grabbing her purse, She opened the door.

"Hey, girl. I was starting to get worried and decided to come look for you. I realized I didn't tell you where exactly in the church the movie would be playing."

"Thanks," She managed feebly. She'd have made her escape if she hadn't gotten distracted.

"No problem. The movie's in the fellowship hall in back." Marla motioned to where the merry trio had disappeared moments earlier. "There's tons of food. The church bought chicken and everyone brought sides. Oh, and you should see the desserts."

"There's a lot of people here." Several cars pulled into the parking lot behind them.

"Yeah. It's a great movie. Plus, they have games and stuff for the kids in another room." Marla waved at a couple about ten years older than her with two small children trailing behind them.

The couple waved back before they walked through double metal doors into a gymnasium-looking space. She searched the sea of faces in the large room they entered. People milled throughout, filling plates with various types of food and chattering exuberantly. The aroma of fried chicken and chocolate intermingled, reminding her how long it'd been since she'd eaten something not quick and cheap.

Jen took up the end of the food line. "What is the movie, anyway?"

"*The Last Dance*," Marla answered as if the name of the movie explained everything.

"*The Last Dance?*" Jen scrunched her nose. How could a movie she'd never heard of before draw so many people? Maybe they were here for the food and free place to hang out.

"Yeah." Marla's gaze pierced Jen as if she couldn't believe her friend hadn't heard of the movie. "You know, the movie about doing everything you can to make a marriage work, never giving up even when it seems over."

Jen blanched. She'd walked into a movie about making relationships work? Why hadn't she asked Marla about the movie on the phone? Now she had to drag her bruised heart through a romance. *And I bet everything works out great for the characters.* "Oh."

Marla blinked several times and rested her hand on her arm. "Oh, Jen. I'm so sorry. I didn't think about it. I forgot about the breakup."

The change in her relationship status on Facebook. Of course Marla had seen it. Obviously she hadn't thought about it in relation to the night's activities. She forced a smile, stepped forward, and grabbed a paper plate. "No, it's fine. Really."

Marla didn't argue or bring it up as they worked their way down the buffet. Jen heaped chicken, macaroni and cheese, broccoli casserole, green beans, and homemade biscuits on her plate. *Guess I'll have to come back for dessert.*

"I don't think there are any seats open at a table. You good with balancing and eating?"

"Yesh." She had already shoved a bite of gooey bread in her mouth.

She looked up and a head of dark hair standing

several inches above most everyone else caught her eye. The mischievous guy from the parking lot. His head tilted back in laughter. The laughter stilled as he lowered his head and his eyes focused on her, but his grin widened.

Jen failed to contain a return smile. She didn't feel like falling for someone again, but she couldn't tear away from his gaze.

He took a step in her direction, but was stopped by someone she couldn't see. He talked to the concealed person, glancing her direction every few seconds. Her cheeks flushed. Did she have no more control over her body that she couldn't force her eyes to look another way?

Marla tugged on her sleeve. "Wanna get a drink? Then we can at least sit and be in place. The movie starts in a few minutes."

Rescued. Thank goodness.

CHAPTER SIX

Jen winced as the onscreen argument between the husband and wife escalated. She jumped when he threw the vase against the wall. As it shattered to the floor, her mind's eye saw a busted phone. Broken picture frames. Pieces of what had once been a remote control.

How many times had her and Ian's disagreements turned volatile? Too many times.

She watched the wife storm out, declaring the marriage over. Why hadn't Jen ever left? Instead, she'd stuck around, picking up the fragments of various material objects while promising herself she wouldn't provoke him next time.

What did the woman in the movie have that Jen didn't?

Probably a mother who didn't remind her that she was a mistake and a failure every chance she got.

Shaking her head, she refocused on the characters. The woman whining to her friends. The man complaining to his.

She watched, mesmerized as things began to change. A soft word here, a thoughtful gesture there. She sat glued to her seat later as the credits ran. Could such simple things really turn that horrible of a relationship around?

If so, it certainly wouldn't take Jesus to do it. The couple were the ones to make different choices. Religion didn't offer answers to real life problems. People needed to rely on themselves. After all, everyone was good deep down. Only mindless, incapable idiots needed some crutch like God to get by day to day.

But it had been religion that worked as the catalyst for change in the couple.

"Jen?"

She looked up. "Yeah?"

"There's a bunch of food left. Wanna check it out? I don't know what it is about movie watching, but it always makes me famished."

Jen giggled. "Me, too. Where's the super-sized, extra-buttered popcorn?"

A twinkle shone in Marla's eyes. "I don't think we have any of that, but I did spot a triple chocolate cake earlier."

"Sounds great."

She split the last gigantic slice with Marla. She spotted Mr. Tall and Mischievous across the room, working his way to the door. Guess she'd never know more about him. Just as well.

"So, Jen, what do you do?" The question from a blonde-headed girl with bright blue eyes drew her into the conversation with Marla's friends. Maybe these people weren't so bad after all.

"I work in accounting. For Pierson."

"I think I've heard of them. They've been in Newport News forever."

"Yeah. A nice, stable, old company. A perfect job."

Marla laughed. "If you call sitting in a cubicle all day every day perfect. I'll take dealing with people over numbers any day."

She rolled her eyes. "And I don't know how you sit through sessions of people spilling their guts all the time."

"It's not so bad."

"Are you from Newport News?"

The old churning returned to her stomach. "No. I grew up in Alabama."

Cute, manicured eyebrows shot up. "Oh, did your

parents move you here? Are you military?"

"No, my folks are still there. I came here to attend Christopher Newport." No need to tell Marla's friend the school's acceptance letter had handed her the ticket the farthest distance from her parents than any other.

"Oh, and you stayed?"

"Yeah, I fell in love with the area." And Ian. And being a thousand miles away from home.

~*~

An hour later as Jen sat in her car outside her apartment in the dark, quiet of midnight, scenes from the night replayed in her head.

The whole evening was drastically different from those she'd had as a child the few times her parents took her to church. On those holiday outings, everything had been stiff and formal. The people at Marla's church hadn't made her feel like an outsider. No one threw darts or arrows or quizzed her about her right to be in a holy building.

She laid her head on the steering wheel and closed her eyes. She'd never thought of God as anything more than a demanding authority. Do this, don't do that. Make sure everything looks good. What she saw this evening contrasted starkly to her view of God.

Swallowing her confusion, she sat up and swung the

car door open. When did life get so complicated? She didn't like confusion.

She loped up the stairs to her apartment. She'd simply forget about tonight. Her life had been perfectly fine without all the Jesus stuff and church people. Without all that, her life would become simple again.

As Jen unlocked her door, the handsome, chiseled face of Mr. Mischievous popped into her mind. *I wish I'd gotten to talk to him.*

Jen closed the door, leaned against it, and slid to the floor. What was it about him? She didn't even know his name and his face sent her heart racing. A week ago she'd been madly in love with someone else.

Had she been in love? The portrait of love in *The Last Dance* was so dramatically different. It wasn't supposed to be about looking for the other person to make her happy. True love looked out for the best interest of the other person. Had she done that with Ian? If she were brutally honest, the answer would be no.

Did that explain why the smile of a new man, one she hadn't even officially met, turned her stomach upside down? If she forgot about tonight, she'd have to put out of mind those dark eyes and jet black hair she'd love to run her fingers through.

No. I'll probably never see him again. She eyed the pile of papers and bills stacked on the kitchen table. *Besides, I can't think about some guy. I've got to find a roommate. Fast.*

She pushed herself up and trudged to the table. She fingered the envelopes and blew a dark lock of hair that'd fallen from her braid out of her eyes. The to-do list she'd made glared at her from beside the pile. Very little had gotten marked off, and the most important had been left untouched. Ignoring the demands crying out from table, Jen mentally swept it all aside, moped down the hallway, and collapsed onto her bed.

She couldn't take another single thought. Her muscles and mind craved sleep. At least that way she'd gain some peace for a while. Everything could wait 'til tomorrow. She closed her eyes and fell asleep picturing dark, twinkling eyes.

CHAPTER SEVEN

A smile crept onto Jen's face as she rolled onto her back and squinted at the sun blaring through her cheap blinds. She stretched and scooted down in the comforter until it met her chin. Nothing had changed, not really, but this Saturday morning felt different.

Mmm. Mr. Tall, Tan and Tantalizing. She didn't think she'd ever seen eyes so dark before. How could she work things to see him again? Meet him, find out his name, anything about him?

Throwing off the covers, she popped out of bed and pulled up the blinds. Outside, sat the same half-full parking lot and worn down playground in the distance. But today the sun shone brightly, reflecting off everything and hitting her square. She stretched again and padded out of her room and down the hallway.

Grabbing a bowl of cereal, she hunkered down on the sofa and flipped on the television.

What was with her? She still had only two weeks to find a roommate or a new place to live. She still had wedding planning books scattered across her room that were now useless to her.

Peaches jumped on her lap, reminding Jen she wasn't utterly alone.

"Hi, Sweetie." She stroked the cat's back with one hand and finished her milky flakes with the other. She laughed as Peaches nuzzled her full hand and set the bowl aside. "Okay, I get it. You missed me. First, you want me gone, now you can't stand to have my attention divided from your precious little self."

The television provided background noise, but she didn't pay attention to what was playing. She buried her head in the exquisitely soft fur and rubbed her feline with both hands.

"What do you think, Peaches? Does today look brighter to you?"

The only answer she got was a deep purr as the tabby circled her lap and settled down.

The stack of papers and bills still lay askew on her dining table. Her eyes lingered on the array. She didn't have to deal with it right away. Not now. It'd all still be there later in the day.

Jen leaned her head against the sofa and closed her eyes. The dark chocolate orbs and captivating grin invaded her thoughts again. Boy, he was cute. But he was also a Christian. How could she even think about being interested in him? The moment he found out she thought God was nothing more than a good idea someone came up with for keeping people in line, he'd turn his gorgeous smile into a growl and flee.

Whatever. If he did, he did. She was doing fine on her own.

Or was she? She eyes popped open and darted to the pile of stress across the room. That's what she called okay?

What was it that struck her so in the movie last night? This morning she could convince herself the confusion it caused didn't exist, but she couldn't deny something in it had made her feel much better. Light. Serene. Is that what religion did? Make people feel souped up and bolster a false sense of life being flaw-free?

She stroked Peaches' fur. At least her cat wouldn't leave her.

The after-glow of a nice evening. An argument-free, drama-free night. Those were the reasons her heart was light and thoughts optimistic this morning.

Hmmm. Monday was trash day. She jumped out of her cozy spot, laughing at Peaches protest, and strode to her room. Time to toss out anything associated with Ian. If nothing else, last night opened her eyes to the narrow escape she'd made.

Pictures still hung on the wall. Their engagement photo lay face down on her dresser. Ticket stubs, menus, and other paraphernalia from years of dating adorned the mirror hanging above her vanity. All of it needed to go.

She lifted the frame atop her chest of drawers and studied it. It was a great picture of her. She'd swept her hair up and sat so the light reflected off her ring perfectly. Pulling the photograph closer, she studied her ex-fiancé. His smile didn't reach his eyes. She had leaned into him, but Ian's back was stiff and straight. Was he really leaning slightly away from her? He was.

How could she have been so blind? He'd been pulling away even as she planned their wedding.

Why had he proposed? Because his parents pushed him to? Because she pushed him to? Everyone had been ready; it seemed like the perfect timing. But he hadn't been.

Passing comments in calm moments came to the forefront of her mind. There was no need to hurry. What would it hurt if they waited? Even the proposal had been under-dramatic. She suggested they go ring shopping, picked out one she liked, and wore it home from the store. He went along with everything.

Not, as Jen had thought, because he was as excited as she was, but because that's who he was.

It didn't matter, now. She dropped the picture, frame and all in the waste basket. All the paraphernalia from her mirror went next, followed by various reminders of misspent time and energy around her room. Every item that reminded her of Ian went in the trash.

About half an hour later, she took the bulging plastic bag outside to the large container. Tears threatened as she threw it in, but Jen shook her head. It was over. As well it should be.

Back inside, her thoughts returned to the evening before. She had so many questions.

She pulled her phone out of her pocket and dialed.

"Hey, Marla? It's me Jen. Are you busy today?"

CHAPTER EIGHT

Jen wrapped her hand around the warm mug and brought the steaming cup to her lips. She sipped it, the warmth flowing down her throat to her stomach and, somehow, radiating out to her fingers and toes. She eyed the half full tables on the small patio. "Whoever heard of eating outside when it's forty degrees?"

Marla laughed, her eyes crinkling. "I know, it's crazy. But they have the best desserts, and it's better than waiting almost an hour for an inside table."

Her thumb played across the top of her cup. "I don't know. This had better be the best cheesecake I've ever had."

"It will be. Isn't the hot chocolate scrumptious?"

"It's good, but at this rate, I'll have to order four cups just to get through one creamy slice."

Marla took a sip and leaned back. "Is that so bad?"

"It is if I want to zip up my pants tomorrow."

"So wear a dress and don't worry about it."

Jen raised her eyebrows. "A dress?"

"Yeah. You're going to come to church with me tomorrow, aren't you?"

"I... I don't know. I hadn't really thought about it."

"You had fun last night, right?"

She smiled. "I did."

"See, you enjoyed yourself."

"Yes, but..."

Marla tucked a stray blonde curl behind her ear. "Yes, but what?"

"I'm not sure about the church thing. Or God for that matter." Jen looked down at her hands, holding the quickly cooling cup. "I mean, I'm not sure I believe in all that."

"Okay. So come to church to find out what it's all about."

"Umm, I don't know." She straightened the spoon and fork next to her cup. "My mom used to make me go to church sometimes and I never got much out of it."

Leaning forward, Marla pushed her cup out of the way to allow the waitress to set down a plate with raspberry and chocolate drizzled cheesecake on the metal table in front of her. An identical slice was placed by her. "Thanks."

The bundled up waitress nodded and left.

Marla turned her attention back to Jen. "Tell me about it."

She shoved a big bite of her dessert in her mouth. The quicker they finished eating, the quicker the conversation ended and she could get out of there. Why had she called Marla this morning?

"Jen?"

She blew out the breath she'd been holding. "My parents took me to church when I was little. Then there was some big blow up, everyone was arguing about something. We left. My mom started going to another church, mostly on holidays, but my dad refused. He said everyone in church was a bunch of hypocrites, and well…" She propped her elbows on the table and looked Marla in the eye. "I kind of agree."

Marla scrunched up her nose and pursed her lips. "I hate when that happens."

She took another bite. Three more and she'd be done. "My mom still goes to church, but I don't see where it's done any good. She still yells at my dad all the time and fusses at me every time we talk."

Playing with the sauces intermingling on her plate, Marla paused before continuing. Her hand stilled and she looked up. "Is your mom kinda rules oriented?"

"You mean like everything has to be a certain way or else?"

"Yeah."

She rolled her eyes. "Always. It's either her way or pay."

"Not much grace in that," Marla mumbled.

"What?" Had she heard her right? Grace?

"Nothing. You know, just because someone who goes to church or claims to be a Christian doesn't act like they should doesn't mean you can't give God a chance."

Jen squished the last bits of her cheesecake between the prongs on her fork and captured the crumbs between her lips. It *was* the best she'd ever had. "I–"

"Hey, there. What are you doing here, Marla?"

She looked up and met the gaze of Mr. Dark Eyes. Her dessert turned to bricks in her stomach. How had she missed him walking up?

"Hey Barrett. Having some delicious dessert with my friend Jen."

He held his hand out. "Nice to meet you. You were at the movie last night."

"Yes." Her hand warmed in his extended embrace. The bricks exploded and somehow became millions of delicate butterflies. He let go and the heat rushed to her cheeks.

"This is my little brother, Bobby." He motioned to the teenage version of himself she hadn't noticed standing next to him. "Mind if we join you?"

Instead of waiting for an answer, he pulled up a chair and sat down. Bobby followed suit.

After ordering another round of hot cocoa, four this time, Marla dug into the second half of her dessert. "So, you guys glutton for frozen toes?"

"Nah." Barrett rubbed his hand over the teen's dark hair. "Bobby earned his driver's permit today and this is his reward."

Marla's eyes sparkled. "You couldn't convince him to take you somewhere indoors?"

Bobby blushed and shrugged.

Jen understood the sentiment. Her mouth felt like she'd been stranded in a desert.

"Bobby wouldn't pick, he was just happy I let him drive." He met Jen's gaze, then eyed the plates. "And I'm a fan of piping hot drinks and succulent desserts."

"Me, too." Marla finished her last bite. "Well, congratulations, Bobby. And we're glad you could join us."

Barrett met Jen's gaze again and she no longer needed

her hot chocolate to warm her. "So, d'ya enjoy the movie?"

"It was…different."

"Your first Christian movie?"

She nodded. How'd he guess? Did she stand out that badly?

"Yeah. They're definitely different than mainstream. It didn't bore you too badly, did it?"

She shook her head. "No. It actually got me thinking."

He raised one eyebrow and leaned in. "That's a good thing, I think. What kind of thoughts did it produce in that pretty little head?"

Pretty? Jen worked her tongue to moisten her mouth. *He said I'm pretty. But he said something else. What was it?*

Oh, yeah. Thoughts. Where had they all gone?

"Hey, if you don't want to talk about it that's okay." Barrett leaned back and picked up his mug.

"No, it's not that. I don't know, I guess I just don't see the point. About God, I mean. The movie seemed to say that if you believe in Him everything will turn out perfect. And I know that's not true."

"No, it's not."

She cocked her head. Had Barrett just agreed with her? "And I've known plenty of people who had long, happy marriages without even a hint of believing in the supernatural."

"Again, true."

"So, what's the point? Isn't God just something to make people feel better about themselves, to shirk responsibility?"

Barrett took a thoughtful sip then set his drink down. "No. I don't see how that would be. God is holy and holds people accountable for their choices, more so than society does. He looks at the heart and intentions. No one can feel good about themselves when their eyes are opened to how they are separated from God."

Her mom certainly fit the description he gave. Nothing was ever good enough. "So God looks down on people and criticizes and judges everything they do wrong. But if He's the one who made us wouldn't it all be His fault?"

Bobby leaned forward. "Yeah. Who wants to follow such a mean God?"

Good. At least she wasn't completely outnumbered.

Barrett grinned.

Had she said something funny? Bobby? A review of their comments didn't reveal a hidden joke.

"He judges people, yes. But in the same way a parent judges a child who's broken a house rule and put himself in danger or gotten hurt. God's rules are to protect us, and just like a parent, He gives them to us because of His love."

Bobby sat back and crossed his arms. "Thanks, but I'd rather figure life out myself. That kind of love is smothering."

A true ally. She couldn't have said it better herself.

"God doesn't want to smother us." Marla spoke up for the first time since the guys arrived. "That's why He gives us options. We can obey or not. We can believe or not."

"Exactly." Barrett's baritone voice sent shivers up Jen's spine.

She squirmed. *How'd I get myself stuck in this deep conversation?*

She met Barrett's penetrating gaze. Enticing coffee eyes. That's what would kept her from dashing away after her last bite of dessert.

"Okay, let's say if there was a God that He would be good and loving. But there's not a shred of proof He exists."

"Does wind exist?"

She narrowed her eyes. What was he trying to get at? "Of course it does."

"How do you know? Can you see it?"

"No, but I can feel it. And see it flapping flags and flipping over plastic chairs."

"Now, would you call that proof of wind or evidence?"

"Evidence. I guess you can't really prove something else isn't causing what I see and feel."

"Right. Now, as for undeniable, inarguable proof that God is real, I can't argue with you there. When I look around, though, I see tons of evidence." He gestured around them. "Do you think these iron tables and chairs were made by creative hands, or thrown together by a storm of molecules."

"Someone made them."

"I agree. Now, which is more complex? This chair?" He leaned forward and gripped the black metal handle of Jen's chair. "Or the person sitting in it?"

She swallowed. Of course she was more complex than a chair. But that didn't prove God existed. She struggled against getting lost in the dark pools of his eyes and losing grasp of the moment and conversation. What was the question again? Something about the chair. And her. Complicated. Oh, things were definitely getting complicated.

He raised his eyebrows.

A response. She needed to answer his question. She gulped again and squeaked, "The person."

CHAPTER NINE

The numbers on Jen's alarm clock glared at her mockingly. Two forty-nine. Her eyes drooped heavily. Her muscles ached from the three-mile run she'd taken after inhaling cold pizza for dinner.

Cocoa, loneliness, and procrastination. That's what had gotten her into trouble. She'd had questions, but never expected the answers to spark new queries in her mind. Jen had left most of them unasked, and they'd been gnawing at her ever since she escaped the cold metal chair and biting wind and slipped into her car. They chased her home, pricked her mind, and distracted her all day.

She tried looking through the paper for roommate ads, quieting her thoughts with a movie, even running. If she couldn't get her mind to shut down, at least she could wear her muscles out and escape through sleep.

Though physically worn out, she'd done nothing but toss and turn since shutting the lights out shortly after midnight. She could blame it on the three cups of hot chocolate and two cups of coffee she'd gulped to stay warm this morning, but caffeine had never affected her sleep before. She'd always bragged she could down a soda or java and be asleep five minutes later.

No, a mild stimulant had nothing to do with her sleeplessness. Rest eluded her because that morning's seemingly inconsequential exchange of ideas about God had pierced holes in what Jen had been sure she knew.

She leapt off the bed and trudged down the hallway. She dug through the cupboard and found a half-empty box of decaf teabags. No reason to take any chances. She grabbed a mug, filled it, and tapped her fingers impatiently as the microwave counted down from sixty. The teabag submerged, She set it on the table beside the sofa, pulled the blanket off the back, and wrapped it around herself.

The questions from her discussion with Barrett, Marla, and Bobby pinged in her mind. The last question plagued her the most. Why, if there really was a God and He really was good and loving, did so many bad things happen? The questions Barrett volleyed back at her had caught her off guard.

Why, given the selfishness, arrogance, and disrespect of people does God continue to love and bless people? Why do people give themselves credit for all good things that come along, say how wonderful they are at making life go on the way they want, and then blame God when a tragedy strikes or dreams crumble?

Jen wanted to argue. Tried to argue. She thought faith was silly. Ignorant, really. God hadn't helped her get into college. Studying hard had. God hadn't gotten her a good job. The results of her efforts towards a degree and interviewing well did.

So why did she blame God when her heart got broken, her roommate moved out and …? No. She wouldn't let her thoughts go there.

Scooping out the teabag and discarding it, she cupped the warm mug in her hands. She saw in Marla and her church friends something she'd never seen before. Logical faith. Faith that asked questions and searched out the answers. Their discussion and responses to her questions hadn't solved anything or sold her yet, but now she couldn't let it rest.

What if she'd been completely wrong? Not only about God's existence, but about what characteristics would make up a perfect God? Her mind longed for more, and in a weak moment she'd accepted the invitation to go to church the next morning.

This morning. Jen checked the time. Three-thirty. She really needed to get some sleep.

Plus, she didn't want to look like a total hag when she got to see Mr. Coffee-eyes again. The curiosity he stirred in her raced side by side with her thirst to know more about his God.

CHAPTER TEN

Jen swallowed the tennis ball-sized lump in her throat and squeezed her eyes shut. The two slices of toast she'd eaten churned in her stomach. Her nerves were as frazzled as her hair would be on a ninety-percent humidity day in July and she'd be mortified if she threw up in front of everyone.

She took a deep breath and headed towards the church entrance. Why was today even more nerve-wracking than when she'd come two days ago for the movie night?

Because you don't believe what these people believe. She braced her shoulders and pushed her feet forward, shaking off her doubts. She was committed now that she'd made it to within twenty feet of the glass doors.

A middle-aged man held one of the doors open and smiled, his crow's feet deepening.

"Good morning."

Jen nodded and shifted her gaze to the floor as she brushed past. *Please, please, please don't ask me any questions.*

She made it past Mr. Cheerful without being quizzed. Walking through the wide corridor, she focused on her feet. She glanced up occasionally to sidestep oncoming foot traffic and ensure she hadn't taken a wrong turn. Every time she peeled her gaze from the floor, smiling faces greeted her. Instead of being filled with warmth and comfort though, the sea of people moving to and from sent tremors through her already sensitive stomach.

Why, oh why couldn't Marla have met her in the parking lot? Her brief text that morning had said something about breakfast, included an apology, and a road map to her Sunday school classroom. If only Marla could have dragged her out of the car and led the way like Friday night. Then she wouldn't have to find her way alone and suffer being gawked at by all these people who were almost certainly wondering about the girl clutching her Bible to her chest and keeping her head down as if she were counting and creating statistics about the tiles and smudges on the floor.

Turn right at the end of the hall, go up the stairs, and it's the third door on the left. The Exit sign hung a few yards ahead, the arrow pointing to the right. That must be the stairs.

Almost there.

How had she gotten into this mess? One cup of cocoa. A few thought-provoking questions.

One tall, dark-haired guy who threw his gorgeous smile out way too quickly.

But she wasn't interested in dating. She wasn't interested in church, either.

Yet here she was.

She paused at the door. Should she turn around and walk back down the hallway she'd just survived going through? Her stomach revolted at the thought. Envisioning herself climbing the stairs and joining a class of goody-two-shoes, know-it-alls-about-religion didn't act as a balm either.

Ascend or backtrack?

"Going up?"

Jen looked into the green eyes of a sandy-blond-haired girl who appeared about sixteen. The teenager held the door open with raised eyebrows.

"Um, yes." Jen thrust her foot over the threshold and began the ascent slowly, allowing Miss Ponytail to bound ahead of her.

She had once been that enthusiastic. That naive. She'd learned better, not to swallow every line thrown her way. Practicality now took precedence over feelings.

So how had she missed the downfall of her

relationship with Ian?

She sighed. *Stomach, please calm down. I simply can't show off my breakfast to everyone this morning.*

She hadn't been this nervous since the first day of high school. The unknown pricked her senses the most. What would it be like? What would be expected of her? Would everyone laugh if she said something stupid?

She'd attended with her aunt a few times when she was really young. It'd been fun, playing games, doing crafts, singing songs, with Bible stories speckled in on occasion. Tales that over the years transitioned to sound more like fairy tales than history.

Surely adult Sunday school would be vastly different. No entertainment or merriment. Just boring discussions between people who couldn't think for themselves. Or worse, everyone sitting sullenly staring at whatever dry, monotone guy was picked to teach the class.

Ugh.

She reached the platform at the top of the stairs and hesitated again. Marla and Barrett weren't like that though. The calculation she'd formed in her mind of Christians didn't add up.

She took a deep breath, pushed through the door and turned left, crashing full force into somebody. The heat rushing to Jen's cheeks intensified as she looked up and took in the wide grin haloed by dark, curly hair.

"Well, mornin'. Wanted to make sure I knew you were here, huh?"

Oh, good grief. I'm going to throw up on him. "I, uh…"

Barrett's strong laugh rippled through the hallway and her veins. "It's okay. I know it's a little anxiety producing being in a new place. I've already grounded Marla for leaving you on your own. So who cares if it was her morning to bring breakfast? We'd have waited."

She stared. Where had all the moisture in her mouth gone?

"I'm heading to the kitchen to get a couple pitchers of water. But I can show you where the room is first." Barrett's hand gently touched her elbow as he guided her the last twenty yards. Suddenly the nausea was replaced with quivers of a different kind. She hadn't known such a delicate touch could wreak so much havoc.

CHAPTER ELEVEN

Marla waved over the dozen or so heads in the room and wove her way through to greet Jen with a hug. "I'm so glad you found it okay. You didn't have any problems, did you?"

She shook her head.

"Great. You hungry? I brought bagels, cream cheese, and a bowl of fruit. There's also juice. Barrett went to get water."

"No, I'm good." She didn't dare tempt her stomach to follow through with its threatening revolt.

"Okay. I want you to meet some people." Marla dragged her by the arm to where two guys and another girl about their age stood.

She nodded to each as Marla introduced her to Cara, Carlos, and Tim.

"Welcome," Carlos said. "It's nice to know Marla has friends. We were beginning to wonder."

Marla punched his arm. "As if. Maybe it's you I'm embarrassed to admit knowing. Ever think of that?"

Carlos draped an arm over Marla's shoulders and crossed his eyes. "Now why would ya go and say a thing like that?"

She blushed. "Oh, I have no idea."

Barrett waltzed in the room with two pitchers of water and Marla slipped away from Carlos' grip to flitter around the snack table.

He watched her walk across the room then turned to Jen. "Seriously, it's nice to meet you. We're glad you could come."

She mumbled her thanks and must have communicated her lack of desire to talk, because he, Tim, and Cara moved onto some small talk she couldn't follow. She'd backed away and scoped out a seat near the door when a guy with spiky blond hair and glasses stood in front of a lone chair dotting the "u" the rest of the seats made.

"All right you rowdy hooligans. Time to get rolling. Fill your plates and cups one more time and take a seat."

The buzzing quieted down as people transitioned to the chairs. Barrett settled down onto a metal chair on the side of the semi-circle opposite Jen. He kicked back and crossed an ankle over his other knee. The perfect picture of relaxation. His eyes left the teacher's direction and met her gaze.

Heat rose to her cheeks and scorched the back of her neck. *Good grief. This is ridiculous.* She nodded at Marla as she sat next to her and trained her gaze on the tall, skinny guy leading the class. He looked more like a basketball player than a Sunday school teacher. She pictured the octopus-like limbs reaching feet above half a dozen heads to snatch a rebound out of thin air.

She stifled a giggle. *Okay. Guess I could at least try to pay attention.* She glanced at Barrett. *Can't look at him. I won't have a clue what was talked about if Marla asks me later.*

Cocking her head and shifting slightly, she focused on Long-Arms.

"So, how can the Bible say God is all-loving, merciful, and compassionate, yet He still sends people to hell and lets evil things keep happening in the world?"

The words blew her back in her chair. She'd said those very words. Wondered those very things. Had Marla prepped the Sunday school teacher? The open book Marla had handed Jen when they sat felt heavier than its thin binding should allow. She looked down at the page the teacher had instructed them to turn to. It held today's date in the bottom right corner. The question Octopus-Limbs asked was printed on the page in black and white.

How in the world?

Maybe it didn't have anything to do with this world.

She sat straighter, primed to hear what answer would be given. Surely these people wouldn't have a problem with anything the Bible said. After all, they were a bunch of flawless, not a care in the world, church-goers. And they would most certainly have the perfect, platitude answer.

"First of all," the teacher continued, "we'll examine the question. Is it the right one?"

"Not really," Barrett's deep voice answered.

Her eyes darted in Barrett's direction. This time, curiosity tamped down her usual reaction.

"The right question is: how can a perfect, holy God accept us?"

They had just said God is loving. Didn't that mean He'll accept people?

You're the one who doesn't think God could love you.

The old argument volleyed in Jen's head. It was easier not to think about all these things. Why had she allowed herself to get stuck here?

"We've all sinned."

Oh, yeah. Those dark eyes and dimpled cheeks.

Barrett continued. "I think we can all agree on that. All of us have broken at least one of God's laws, most of us several. And multiple times. We wouldn't expect a judge to let someone go without punishment when they break a law, that wouldn't be just."

Barrett was such a jokester. Even though they'd gotten into some discussion over hot chocolate the day before, she still didn't expect this guy who laughed so easily to get so serious.

The discussion pinged around the room as Jen sat quietly, taking it all in. Was there a reason she was here on this particular day? What were the chances the preplanned topic of discussion would match her exact doubts?

Coincidence. Had to be.

Her head spun as the class discussed God's goodness, people's badness, justice, and fairness. It actually began to make sense.

God was perfectly good and loving. People fell short of God's perfection, living self-centered lives with a trail of destruction behind them. To be absolutely just, the Lord had to hold people accountable for their choices. But because He's merciful, he sent Jesus to pay the penalty for all sin.

"I heard someone explain it like this," Carlos spoke

up. "Jesus is like a lawyer who stands in front of the great judge and says, 'Don't punish them for what they've done wrong, I paid the price. I set them free.' He offers his forgiveness not because we deserve it. We never could. He offers it because of his goodness."

Jen had never thought about God in those terms. But what about the bad stuff that happened?

A few minutes later, a girl she hadn't met asked almost that exact question. "If God's so good, though, what about all the evil? You still haven't answered the initial question."

The teacher leaned forward and rested his elbows on his knees. "In a way, you're right, Gretchen. But in a way we did. God allows things to happen that we consider bad when it will ultimately draw someone closer to Him or bring Him glory. Pain, sorrow, tragedy, and disasters are all part of the consequences of sin. The whole world was affected when Adam and Eve chose to go their own way."

Barrett nodded. "That's right, and only a holy God could take all of sin and its consequences and turn them into good."

Everything Jen thought made sense got stirred up again. Would it all come together? The conversation continued, as she sorted out what she'd already heard.

Before she knew it, time was up.

Octopus-Arms checked the time on his phone. "Alright folks, time's up. Let's close."

He bowed his head. "Lord, direct us to You and open our eyes to Your truth. Let us not hold fast to our traditions and beliefs if they don't glorify You. Reveal any deception we've accepted. Thank You for Your perfect, eternal love. Amen."

Marla rose with the rest of the group and turned to Jen. "So, you didn't have snack at the beginning. Does that mean you'll join us for lunch?"

She inhaled and assessed her stomach's rumblings. Nope. Queasiness was gone. The gurgling must mean it was ready to accept food again.

Marla leaned in before she had a chance to answer. "Barrett's going."

Heat rushed to her cheeks once again. She could lie and say it didn't change anything. Her thumping heart shouted the truth. She'd love to go. Her thinning wallet and sensible side argued with her feelings. "I don't know if I should."

"Come on, we haven't had a chance to talk today. Not really."

She opened her mouth to answer, then jumped when

an arm fell across her shoulders.

"So, you going to lunch with us?" Barrett's dimples shone.

"Um, yeah." *What? Did I just agree to go?*

"Great. That's where we usually finish class. Forty-five minutes isn't near enough to get through a whole lesson."

Her tongue stuck to the roof of her mouth. His touch sent streaks of lightening throughout her body, which should have revitalized her ability to speak, but it didn't.

Now she'd not only have a chance to spend more time around Barrett, but also ask the questions rebounding in her head. If she mustered up enough courage.

Did she really need courage, though?

No one had attacked her. No one had jumped down anyone's throat when they disagreed with an idea or opinion. She felt…comfortable with these people. Which shocked her more than her attraction to Barrett.

His arm popped off her shoulders. "All right, see you there." He spun around and strolled out of the room.

Out of the room, but not out of her life. She'd see him again in a few minutes. A grin took over her face as she followed Marla down the steps.

CHAPTER TWELVE

Jen strolled across the parking lot humming an unfamiliar tune. She didn't take the time to figure out the words to the music; she was too busy mulling over the previous day. Church hadn't been as bad as she'd expected.

A smile emerged. Especially Barrett.

But, I've sworn off dating. I can't let my heart get pummeled again.

She didn't have to go there. It wasn't as if he'd asked her out. He'd simply been funny and kind and amiable. She could simply enjoy his company as a friend.

Guess that means I'll be going back to church.

A sigh escaped as she pushed through the double glass doors labeled 'Pierson Accounting' into the two-story steel, concrete, and glass building. Another day of certainty. Numbers were always predictable. That's why she loved accounting. Facts and figures. Formulas and calculations. They did what they were supposed to. They never got confused or forgot to call.

She nodded to the couple of coworkers already at their cubicles as she wove her way to her own. Glancing at her watch, she knew the coffee pot wouldn't be full for a few more minutes. Marty always turned it on at seven-forty and it took five minutes to brew.

Consistency, even in the way the office ran.

Her computer screen came alive exactly forty-two seconds after she pushed the power button. Jen typed in her password, still humming. Opening Outlook, she browsed the pile of emails from the weekend. She deleted the spam and opened a couple of work related messages. Not really anything she needed to know. She dumped those in the trash as well. The next one down the list caught her eye. Sara's message had come from her personal address.

That's odd. She checked the time. It'd been sent Friday night. After work hours. *Maybe that explains why she sent it from home. But why to everyone in the office?*

Her eyes widened as she read the email's contents.

> *Beware. I was asked to stay after work to talk with the GM. I was "fired" because of lack of performance. Things are bad and*

they've kept it quiet. I did some digging and the company's crashing. I won't be the last one to go.

Sara

Her heart sped up. What was going on? She'd worked at Pierson Accounting since college, having started part time during her junior year. They hadn't hesitated the slightest in making her full time when she'd graduated. Surely she'd know if something was up.

Sara had only worked there for a little over a year. This was only her side of what happened. She must have done something. Pierson never let anyone go without cause.

Glancing around, she noticed the few others at work early chatted light-heartedly around the office. Maybe no one had checked their email yet. She reread the ominous warning. Clicking the delete button, she sat back.

I'll be fine.

With everything else that had crumbled in her life the past week and a half, she couldn't contemplate losing her job.

What is it people say about bad things happening in three's?

She shook her head. She wouldn't go there. Nothing was wrong. She attempted to resume the merry tune she'd been humming minutes before, but the melody had vanished from her working memory. She closed her email.

The aroma of gourmet coffee tugged at her nose. She grabbed the brown mug with pink letters stating, "Coffee before anything," and slipped out of her desk.

Marty stood by the coffee pot, filling his cup. His eyes darted behind her. She glanced back and saw no one close by. He leaned forward and spoke in a hushed tone. "You read the email?"

"Yes. What's up?"

"Not sure. I've been hearing rumors, though. Ever since the big boss retired last year with his ginormous bonus, things have gotten shaky."

Jen poured the steaming liquid into her mug and doctored the dark concoction with flavored creamer and real sugar. She couldn't stand that artificial stuff. "How bad?"

Marty shrugged. "Who knows? But the GM and COO have been locked in the conference room since before I got here."

"So tell me more about these rumors."

"Apparently, Mr. Evans' math skills didn't transfer into management. I knew he made a good salary, but I always wondered about his house in the islands."

She sipped the creamy liquid. "The islands? I knew about a place in Florida. His wife spends three months there every winter, right?"

"Right. But apparently some funds had been siphoned off for the last ten years to a mortgage company in Turks and Caicos."

"Whoa."

"Exactly. Word has filtered out over the last few months and clients are jumping ship."

Marty had been at Pierson for over ten years. His wife had worked there until they had their first child a few years back. He probably knew the ins and outs more than anyone. And she trusted him.

"I have noticed shrinking client lists. How come we haven't heard anything in the office?"

Marty leaned his thin frame against the counter. "They've kept it all hush-hush. Trying to fix everything Evans left broken without doing more damage."

"But?"

"You know how it goes. One person tells another, who tells a friend and before you know it the leak grows."

"So how'd you find out?"

"My uncle's a client. Actually, *was* a client."

She whistled low. "Well, I–"

"Jen?"

She turned to see the GM, perfectly attired in his Brooks Brothers suit and silk tie, standing in the doorway.

"Yes?"

"Can I see you for a minute?"

She glanced at Marty, then back at the door. "Um, sure."

Her heart raced as she followed the balding pinstriped suit to the conference room. Her insides shook and mind darted to the upcoming rent. They couldn't fire her. They just couldn't.

CHAPTER THIRTEEN

With shaking hands, Jen collected her personal belongings from her desk. Did she dare take the time to pull her personal files off the computer? Glancing over her shoulder at the floor manager glaring from the doorway of his office answered her question.

Yesterday her favorite supervisor, today her enemy. How could he chat with her in the break room, make jokes after staff meetings for years, and now coldly meet her gaze as she gathered her personal belongings and vacated the building 'within ten minutes'? "Fine."

She fought the tears threatening to spill and scooped the change out of her top drawer, dumping it in her purse.

Marty met her gaze over his cubicle. His eyes soft, he mouthed, *I'm sorry*. She nodded. Maybe she could message him later and see if he could send her the files from her computer. She snatched her packages of crackers and candy from the middle drawer. The last item to gather was her framed picture of Peaches. She held the photo to her chest.

All I have left.

Her nose burned and eyes brimmed. Shaking her head, she gulped. *I won't fall apart in the office and give those heartless managers the satisfaction.*

She lifted her chin, rolled her shoulders back, and marched out. She drove home on auto-pilot, not remembering much of the drive by the time she pulled into her parking spot.

Now she'd lose her apartment for sure. What was she going to do? Go home to live with her parents?

She shivered. Absolutely not. Moving back to Alabama simply wasn't a viable option.

For now, she'd trudge up to her apartment and bury her woes in Peaches' soft fur. And maybe look through the stack of newspapers for a job instead of a roommate.

Jen unlocked her apartment door and stepped in. Her phone vibrated and she dropped her keys fumbling for it beneath all the things stuffed in her purse from her desk. Peaches sprinted out from her bedroom as she kicked the door closed with her foot and answered the incessant ringing.

"Hello?"

"Hey, it's Marla. You okay? You sound like you just finished a five-k."

"Yeah. Well, no, not really."

"What's up?"

"I..." Her throat constricted. She swallowed back the ever-threatening tears. "I can't really talk right now."

"I was calling to see if you wanted to grab lunch. Want me to come pick you up? I'm just a couple blocks away."

Peaches circled Jen's ankles, purring and begging to be picked up. "No. I'm not at work."

"Are you sick? We can always meet another day. I could bring you some soup or something after I get off."

"No." She struggled to gain control. "They fired me. Said I wasn't 'performing my duties well.'"

"Oh, Jen, I'm so sorry. You have to meet me for lunch. My treat."

"No, really. You don't have to. I'll be alright."

"I insist. Wanted to see you today anyway. And now it seems like you'll have even more to talk about."

Even more? Did I have something to talk about already?

She sat and stroked Peaches back. It'd be foolish to turn down a free meal at this point. Plus, Marla always cheered her up. "Thanks. Where do you want me to meet you?"

"Chimi's."

"Okay. I'll be there at twelve." She ended the call and laid her head back on the door.

What would she have done if Marla didn't continue to randomly call her? Lately, it seemed she called Jen exactly when she needed to talk.

Of course, she had done quite of bit of her own contact initiating. What had possessed her to reconnect with Marla in the first place?

Oh, yeah. Boredom and loneliness. Now that had led to a good friend…one she needed.

And Barrett.

A smile crept onto her face. Okay, maybe she didn't have *nothing*.

The conversations from the last two days rushed back. She'd tried to convince herself God didn't exist. The truth was clear now. She'd been angry at Him, blaming the God she'd learned about as a young child for every bad thing that had ever happened to her. She'd denounced Him because He hadn't worked everything out the way she desired.

Different parents would have been nice. She'd also have appreciated some solid protection as a young girl.

How about now? Everything in Jen's life was disintegrating. Maybe God was taking everything away from her because she'd turned away from Him. She deserved punishment.

She sighed and laid her head on her open palm.

Reconnecting with Marla happened at the perfect time. The random, universal invitation to a free movie on the exact night she had to get out of the house to keep from going crazy.

Then meeting Barrett. She wasn't quite sure about that timing, as her determination to not get involved with another guy any time soon remained firm. However, he'd kept her thinking and laughing since they'd been introduced. Her smile perked back up.

Maybe she needed to start focusing on what she had instead of zeroing in on the negative.

At the top of the list? Her new friends.

Her gaze landed on the chaos on the table across the room and her smile drooped.

Having new friends was great, but it wouldn't pay the rent.

CHAPTER FOURTEEN

"Did you have any warning?"

Jen popped a salsa laden chip in her mouth and shook her head. "Not really. A coworker gave me a heads up when I arrived this morning, and things have been a little odd lately, people there one day and not the next. But none of the management ever said anything to me. Not even a single reprimand."

"They fired you for lack of performance, but they've let other people go, too?"

She nodded. "Yeah. I don't call that getting fired, I call it getting laid off."

"Me, too." Marla paused as the waitress delivered two plates brimming with burritos, enchiladas, rice, and beans. "Are you gonna fight it?"

"I'm not sure." Jen's shoulders slumped and every

muscle felt three times as heavy. Did she have energy to argue?

"I think you should. If they're letting a bunch of people go, you have a right at least to unemployment. The only reason they're calling it 'fired' is to avoid paying out."

"I know, but even if I had any idea of what to do or who to report them to, I don't have time to do anything about it. If I don't get a job within the week it won't matter." She stirred her salad with her fork. "A job and a roommate."

Looking up, Marla raised her eyebrows. "What?"

"My roommate had to move home a couple weeks ago because of a family emergency and so far, I haven't found a replacement. Even with my job I couldn't make rent by myself."

"Oh, Jen. Why didn't you tell me?"

She shrugged. "I don't know. I didn't want to seem like a complainer."

"That's not complaining, that's sharing what's going on in your life." With a twinkle in her eye, Marla grinned and sat back.

Was her plight amusing? She stared.

"I have an idea."

"Okay…."

"I live in an above garage apartment at my parent's. It

has two bedrooms and I'm there all by myself. Why don't you come live with me?"

Jen's mouth fell open. "I–" She what? Her brain hadn't had time to process losing her job, much less working out her living situation. What if she could find a job within the week? And a roommate? She liked Marla, but move in with her? Closing her mouth, she dropped her shoulders.

She couldn't kid herself any longer. Finding a new job in a week in this economy would be less likely than a kindergartener writing out pi to the trillionth place.

Suddenly have new roommates banging down her door? Her chances were about as good as the Dow reaching a hundred thousand by week's end.

"Thanks, I don't know what to say. I need time to think."

"I understand. It's been a horrible day. Sounds like an awful month. Here's the deal, I'll draw up a rental agreement. The first month will be free, and we'll set a fee based on whatever job you get. Oh, and we'll look into where to report your getting laid off together."

She stilled her fork. "I…wow."

~*~

The pile of bills surrounded Jen on the floor. She'd paid every one she could and calculated how much she'd have left after her final paycheck. Tears filled her eyes. Once she paid the fee for getting out of her lease early, she'd only have a couple hundred dollars left. And she knew more bills would come after she shut everything off. Then there was her cell bill. She'd just signed a new contract. No way could she cancel that and pay the outrageous get-out-of-contract charge.

She stood and paced around the papers. She puckered her mouth and narrowed her eyes. How dare those cowardly liars sack her? And tell her she wasn't doing her job. Just six months before she'd gotten recognition at an annual reception for outstanding work.

Peaches raised her head from her perch on the back of the sofa.

"I know, I know. Getting mad doesn't change anything."

Peaches licked her paw.

"It doesn't get me a new job or my old one back, as if I'd even take it right now."

She had no choice. She had to leave. And she couldn't afford to move anywhere else that charged rent.

Marla's offer loomed in front of her.

So did one other thought. Moving back to Alabama and her parents' house. Jen shook her head and groaned.

Not a possibility. She refused to give her mother the opportunity to take over her life again.

No other option existed. She'd take Marla up on her proposition.

Peaches leapt off the couch and bounded over the piles of paperwork to rub against her leg. "Meow."

"I don't want to leave either." She scooped up her cat and rested her cheek against the soft fur. What would it take to pack up her life and completely rearrange it? How would she put the pieces back together without having a clue as to what would come next?

CHAPTER FIFTEEN

Jen bit her lip and shuffled the box in her arms to keep from dropping it. Heat rose from her stomach to her neck and cheeks. How could this happen? She'd lost almost everything, and now that things looked better, or at least an option opened up superior to being homeless or moving back with her parents, it came with a huge price. Higher than she wanted to pay.

"I'm so sorry."

She shook her head and gulped. "I should have asked. I just…Peaches is such a huge part of my life. I never thought about you being allergic."

Marla sneezed. "If my allergies weren't so bad, I really wouldn't mind. I love cats, I just can't breathe around them. Or see. My eyes get so itchy, red, and watery. I really wish I'd said something."

"I should have asked." Jen swallowed. Then what? She wouldn't have agreed to move in with Marla and she'd be stuck with nowhere to go.

"I'm really sorry."

She nodded and shuffled to the empty bedroom. She dropped the box of books, and sank on the floor beside it. Her nose burned and tears threatened to spill over her eyelids. How in the world could she give up Peaches?

Why hadn't she thought to ask if it was okay to bring her cat? Everything had happened so fast. The tornado-like changes in her life over the last three weeks had obviously robbed her of critical thinking skills.

What would she do? She couldn't leave her out on the street, couldn't take her to a shelter with the chance she wouldn't be adopted, but… No. Jen shook her head and one lone tear burned its way down her cheek. Her cat waited patiently in the car to be unloaded like all of her other belongings.

"You okay?"

She jerked out of her thoughts and looked at the doorway to see Marla watching her sympathetically. Sighing, she stood and shrugged. The lump in her throat proved an impenetrable barrier to any words.

"You ladies gonna help unload all this stuff or stand

around gabbin' while the guys do all the heavy lifting?" Barrett's jovial voice boomed from behind Marla only a moment before he bumped her out of the way. He carried the headboard and footboard to her bed. "Box springs and mattress are next. You girls game?"

He set the antique wooden pieces down and turned, meeting her gaze. "What…"

Marla answered the unfinished question. "It's Jen's cat. I didn't know she had one and she didn't know I'm severely allergic."

"Oh." His soft brown eyes held Jen's attention.

Her stomach warmed and she looked down. Why did this man cause such a reaction in her, even when grieving the loss of everything important to her?

"You know, our house has been cat free for a little over a year. I think it's high time my mom replaced Skittles. She needs someone to take care of."

Jen looked up.

"Other than me, Bobby, and my dad. We sure could use an attention break." He winked at her.

"Really?" Her heart leapt. Peaches could live with someone she knew? Someone she'd love to have an excuse to get to know better? To go visit on a regular basis?

"Really."

She restrained herself from lunging across the room and throwing her arms around his neck. She halted the image of planting a humongous thank-you smacker right on his lips. Instead, she relaxed her shoulders, offered a lop-sided grin, and said, "Thanks. That'd be phenomenal."

CHAPTER SIXTEEN

Jen stared at the blank sheet of paper in front of her. Thirty minutes and she hadn't been able to string five words together. *Dear Mom and Dad,* That's it.

She hadn't talked to her parents in so long. Their last words had been shouted. Still, she needed to at least tell them she'd moved. Should she also tell them she'd lost her job, her cat, her fiancé? Humph. They hadn't even known she'd been engaged. Tears brimmed in her eyes. At least now she wouldn't have to figure out whether to invite them to her wedding or not.

So, she could definitely leave that tidbit out. She scrawled out two sentences. One saying she'd moved. The other including her new address.

Not that it mattered. She hadn't so much as gotten a Christmas card from them in four years. How to sign it?

Certainly not "love." Just her name.

The brief note folded and stuffed, she licked the envelope and stamped it. Better slip it into the mailbox before she had a chance to think on it more.

Back in the garage apartment, Jen stood in the middle of the tiny living room and looked around. What should she do now? When had she found herself with this much free time?

Never.

She plopped on the sofa and started to call for Peaches to join her, then remembered.

She sighed and played with the fringes of the afghan housed on the back of the sofa. Maybe it wouldn't be too soon to go visit her favorite feline. The corners of her lips turned up. Digging her phone out of her back pocket, she checked the time. Not quite four. He wouldn't be home until six. She had no desire to sit around by herself for several more hours. At least unpacking had kept her busy the last few days.

She'd go out for a paper. Get a cup of coffee. Go through the want ads and work on her résumé. That'd help her fill the empty time.

Jen popped off the couch, strode to her new bedroom, grabbed her keys and laptop, and headed out the door.

Less than thirty minutes later, she'd commandeered a table at the local gourmet coffee shop. Several jobs looked promising, although chances were good the competition would be tough. Time to work on polishing her vita. Maybe being at the same company since she was a junior in college would help.

Her phone chimed with a text. Marla, offering to meet for dinner. How much charity could she take?

Get real. Without Marla's help you'd be homeless or groveling to your parents. Things will change, you'll get back on your feet, and you'll be able to pay her back.

She tapped off her response and glanced at the clock in the bottom right hand corner of the screen. Twenty minutes. Maybe she'd wait until after seeing Peaches to work on her résumé. She'd be in a better mood then, anyway. A full stomach, snuggling with her kitty…and time with Barrett. Jen closed her laptop, folded up the paper, and sprinted to her car.

CHAPTER SEVENTEEN

Her nose buried deep in Peaches fur, Jen inhaled the scent of feline. She grinned and loosened her grip, stroking the fur she'd missed so much over the last few days. Sitting back, she relished the little paws dancing on her lap before settling down and curling under the mass of affection.

"I think she's missed you." Barrett's grin sent a whole new type of warmth through her.

"I hope so. I've certainly missed her." Jen glanced up and the brief meeting of gazes caught her breath in her throat. *Really, Jen? Get a grip on yourself.* She lowered her eyes to the safety of her cat.

The silence in the room surrounded and infiltrated her. Unlike most times the noise of life halted, this came with a comfort. She braved raised eyes and met Barrett's. "What?"

"Nothing. Just letting you process."

"How'd you know?"

"That's my secret. For me to share, you have to agree to share a secret, too."

Never. She could never tell Barrett all her secrets. Her hurts. Disappointments. Choices. Someone like Barrett wouldn't understand. "Secrets?"

"You know, what makes you tick. Dreams you've never shared with anyone."

She stroked Peaches' ear, mulling over his question. What made her tick? She simply got through every day. Dreams? Beyond fanaticizing about her wedding and being married, she hadn't dared let herself imagine good things for the future. Not since…

Her heart sped up. She hadn't thought about that in the longest time. She couldn't share. Barrett would think she was crazy. She shrugged.

"Okay, I'll let you off the hook for now, but I won't forget." He stood and held a hand out. "Now, come."

"Come? Where?"

"I have a theory."

Jen raised her eyebrows. What in the world? She stirred and Peaches leapt off her lap. Reaching out, she took his hand and ignored the tingling in her stomach.

He led her around the chair she'd unfolded

herself from to the bay window behind it. He flipped a light switch and pulled the shade up.

"Is that…?"

"Yep, snow."

"Oh, no. I've got to go. It's starting to stick."

"Not yet." He held tight to her hand when she attempted to pull it away. "Look at it. Watch it."

Taking a deep breath, she exhaled and focused on the snow falling against the backdrop of a streetlight. It glistened. Floated.

"Did you ever make paper snowflakes in school?"

She grinned. "Of course."

"And what did you learn about them?"

"That every single one is different." She scrunched up her nose. "Not sure who gathered bunches of snowflakes on a frozen platform to study them and figure that out, though."

Barrett chuckled. "Me either. But isn't each one beautiful?"

She examined the flow of sparkling white dots. "Yeah."

"That's how God feels about each of us. We're all different, made to be unique among millions. He knows the intricacies of our makeup and loves us each. Isn't that amazing?"

Looking back, she saw the sincerity in his eyes. She could almost believe when he talked about God.

If only she didn't know what she knew. If only it wasn't for those secrets. The things she'd done. The things that had been done to her.

She looked back out the window, the glimmering in her eyes blurring the snow. "Yes. That would be amazing."

CHAPTER EIGHTEEN

The snow continued to drift down as she stared out the window. The white drops drifted down gently, but steady enough to cover the walkway and her car parked by the curb. She smiled as a handful of teenagers ran by, one pulling the other on a skateboard.

They raced down the street out of view and she refocused on the snow covering the front stoop and steps. Each flake unique. Just like each person.

How did that happen?

She'd never considered the question before. She'd simply lived her life as she desired, never stopping to contemplate the existence of a Deity who might actually care about her and the decisions she made.

It was easier that way, wasn't it? Doing what she wanted, ignoring the possibility she'd one day be held accountable for those choices.

She had to admit, though, it hadn't gotten her what she wanted. It'd left her with a broken heart, lost job, homeless, and almost desperate enough to contact her parents for help.

A shiver ran up her spine. Thank goodness Marla and Barrett had stepped in to carry her through.

Thank goodness, or thank God?

She could accept there was God or some kind of higher being who'd created everything. But a Father who loved her completely? Who made her uniquely like she was on purpose?

She shook her head. She couldn't solve the world's greatest mystery tonight. Besides, when she turned and met Barrett's gaze again, all other thoughts vanished.

"So, hot chocolate, hot tea, or coffee?"

"Um…what?"

"You didn't drive all the way over here to spend five minutes with Peaches and leave did you?"

"No, I – is it all right?"

Barrett laughed. "Of course. My folks will be back from a meeting soon. I thought we might watch a movie or something. Then you'll get even more snuggle time."

She envisioned curling up next to Barrett, tucked

under his arm. Heat rose to her cheeks. "Sure."

"Great. You go find your furry friend while I get the drinks."

Oh, right. Snuggling with the cat. Her cheeks blazed. Good thing he couldn't read her thoughts. She hoped.

He walked across the room, stopped, and turned back. "You never did say what you'd like to drink."

"Tea."

"Okay, I'll be right back."

She sank onto the sofa and clicked her tongue several times. Peaches came running and leapt into her lap. "Guess you'll be the one keeping me cozy tonight."

A few moments later, Barrett returned and set down a steaming cup on the table next to her. He placed a second scorching mug on the table at the opposite end before walking over to the entertainment center and opening the cabinet on the left. "So, comedy, thriller, or classic?"

"Thriller."

"Okay." He browsed a few more minutes then snatched a case.

She stroked Peaches back. "So, what are we watching?"

Barrett grinned. "A surprise."

"I've never heard of that one."

His laugh filled the room.

"You're really not going to tell me?"

"No."

He slid the disc in, sat in the other recliner, and aimed his gaze and captivating smile right at her. Jen's stomach knotted. How could this man affect her so with only his presence? She looked away and focused on the opening credits. Peaches purred.

She couldn't remember the last time she felt this content. Comfortable. She curled her legs underneath her and cupped her mug in both hands, the liquid finally cool enough to sip. If this was God, setting all this up, taking care of her when the bottom fell out of absolutely everything, maybe she should give Him a second thought.

CHAPTER NINETEEN

Jen closed her phone and hopped off the sofa, pacing in Marla's miniscule den. She twirled. Two days. She had an interview in two days. Not a job she ever anticipated, but a possibility nonetheless. When she sent out over thirty applications in the last week after moving in with Marla she never expected the one response to be for a church secretary position. How ironic.

Maybe it wouldn't be too bad. Answering phones wasn't exactly challenging. She knew computers well enough and all the programs listed as requirements in the job description. It would even include a little accounting. She grinned. It was a job, and the only prospect she had at the moment.

She stopped and surveyed Marla's simple décor. Pale blue sheers over the windows, a blue plaid sofa and love seat, glass-topped coffee table. One wall held a handful of framed photos. She smiled at the capturing of Marla with various family and friends. In one she wore a cap and gown flanked by her parents. In another she donned a swimsuit and life jacket in a kayak with another girl appearing to be the same age.

She glanced over the next couple then stopped at the larger picture to the right of the others. She stepped closer to inspect the photo. A young girl, about ten, held a baby boy in her arms, sitting on a porch swing. Same blonde hair and big brown eyes as Marla, it must be her. But who was the baby? She didn't have a little brother as far as Jen knew. A cousin maybe?

After pondering the picture, and the possibility of asking Marla about it later, she moved on to the opposite wall. She'd noticed the adornments before, but hadn't taken the time to examine them. The words stenciled on the wall captured her attention first.

"Let your unfailing love surround us, Lord, for our hope is in you alone. Psalm thirty-three, twenty-two."

Unfailing love. That would be nice. Did it really exist? So far, not in her life. Everyone had let her down. Asked too much in return. Her parents. Her fiancé. Her employer. Numerous others who'd lied, broken promises, ignored her needs.

If a love that never failed did exist, she was certain it would take some kind of deity.

Around the painted quote, several crosses varying in size and designs hung in the general shape of an oval. By all appearances, from Marla's apartment and her life, she really believed all this stuff. Truth be told, Jen had thought more about God in the few days since reconnecting with her college acquaintance than in the entirety of her life.

She'd thought more about her relationship with her parents and Ian, too. She fingered one of the more ornate crosses as she remembered the times her mother had yelled at her, called her names, reminded Jen how worthless she was. Tears brimmed her eyes. She never measured up to her mother's expectations. Her father had been too uninvolved and busy avoiding her mom to ever pay her any attention. Then, the incident.

She shook at the memory. Even then her parents hadn't stood up for her, protected her. They'd blamed her and shoved it in a box, duct taped it, and shoved it to the back of a closet, never to be spoken of again.

Is that why she threw herself so completely into Ian's arms when he'd shown her the slightest positive attention?

Crossing her arms, she held on to them protectively. Had anyone ever truly looked out for her interest? Pam. She had been a Christian, too. A real one.

She hadn't been judgmental. Neither were Barrett, Marla and their friends. They were kind, thoughtful, funny, giving, and sincere. Jen wasn't sure she was ready to adopt everything they believed, but she was willing to keep listening. And watching.

Letting go of the grip she had on her arms and turning from the wall display, she strode across the room and down the short hall to the bathroom. Her habit of late, taking a shower by the time Marla was due home from work, would have to be adjusted if she actually got this job. She reached in the stall and turned on the water.

What else would have to change?

Her wardrobe. That's the second thing she'd have to change. Jen held the turquoise top to her, spun around and threw it on the pile of discards heaped on her bed. She didn't have room for all these clothes anyway. Most of them had been pulled out of boxes over the last hour since she'd received the call.

She'd gotten the job. They hadn't even waited the two days they'd told her to expect after her interview. They'd called her a day early. Two weeks exactly after she'd gotten fired she had a new job. And she started on Monday. Only four days to pull herself together.

She snatched up a pair of gray slacks and slipped them on a hanger next to a conservative pink blouse. She'd worn business casual at her last job, but they didn't mind tight and low cut. The church office probably would. At this point, though, she really didn't care. She was once again employed and wouldn't have to rely on charity anymore.

She deflated onto the bed next to the growing mound of material. She wouldn't have an excuse to live with Marla anymore. The heaviness of her stomach and ache in her heart surprised her. She'd only lived there a couple weeks, but it already felt like home. Was she ready to venture out on her own again? Find an apartment? A new roommate? Although she'd have a paycheck, it still wouldn't be enough to live by herself.

A picture of Peaches caught her eye. A grin peaked out from her previously pursed lips. She should be overjoyed at the prospect of getting her beloved feline back full time, but instead tears sprung to her eyes. She'd lose her new friend and excuse to go visit Barrett on an almost daily schedule.

Her phone buzzed. A new message from Marla, "Hey! Hear you got the job. Yay! Dinner on me 2nite 2 celebrate."

Marla should be grateful to get rid of the freeloader she felt like. But here she was offering another dinner out. A real smile broke through. Of course, after the one meal Marla had cooked for them last week, Jen was doubly grateful. If that girl had to rely on her own cooking for nourishment, she'd be a stick.

She tapped off a reply. "Thanks. Won't have 2 support me much longer."

"No prob. And don't even think ur moving out. I'd b bored 2 death."

She gaped at the screen. Marla didn't plan on giving her the boot at first chance. Her world wasn't going to get tossed by another storm, one she might drown in this time. The seas ahead looked calm.

And she knew just where they should celebrate. "Thx my friend. 6@Seaside?"

"Perfect."

Dinner plans. A warm, inviting place to live. A great roommate. Peaches taken care of by Mr. Mischievous with dimples. A new job. She'd have never believed everything could come together for her again. How had that happened?

Did God really care? Had He played a role in the details of her life smoothing back out?

She stood and crossed the room in two and a half steps. She lifted the picture frames and miscellaneous decorating items out of an opened box and stacked them on her dresser. She reached for the final remaining object. The Bible she'd resisted throwing out when she left her apartment. She ran her hand over the cover. What book had Marla recommended she read? Something-uns. What was it?

She opened the cover and found the table of contents. Two Corinthians. Galatians. Ephesians. Philippians. Colossians. Two Thessalonians. It had to be one of those. She closed her eyes. Which one? She should have written it down. Her eyes popped open and her finger rested in the middle. Colossians. She'd start there. After all, according to the page count, it was a small book. That worked for her. She inhaled deeply and flipped the pages.

CHAPTER TWENTY

Closing and setting the Bible aside, Jen pushed herself off the sofa. She strode across the room, once again studying the array of crosses on the wall. What if it were all true? That would change everything.

She fingered one of the smaller, more ornate ones. The words she'd read in the book of Colossians unlocked and flung open the information-filled drawers of her mind.

She'd kept the ancient book her aunt had given her. She'd hung the cross necklace she'd received at a Bible club years before on her review mirror. Yet she had sealed the verses, the references to God, the trappings of religion in the far regions of her mind's storage. Filed under the heading "extraneous."

She slipped her phone out of her back pocket and checked the time. Ten after five. Barrett should be home from work and she didn't need to leave to meet Marla for another half hour. She scrolled to his number and hit send. His deep, baritone voice answered after two rings.

"Hey, Jen."

"Barrett. I was afraid you'd be busy. Can you talk?"

"Whoa. Sounds serious. You alright?"

She pushed a lock of hair out of her face. "Yes, I'm fine. I think."

"You think?"

"Yeah, I have some more questions." She inhaled a gulp of air. "I read Colossians."

Silence filled the line.

"Barrett?"

"I'm here. Just thinking. Interesting place to start. Not the book I'd have suggested."

Heat rushed to her cheeks. "It was small."

"No, nothing's wrong with it. It's just…."

"Heavy."

His deep laugh rang clear. "Yeah. Not exactly a light reading exercise."

"So, is it true? I mean, it's so different from what I've always thought religion was about."

"The short answer is yes." He hesitated, then continued. "You had specific questions, though?"

"It talks so much about freedom. That it's not all about rules and thou shall nots."

"No, it really isn't. So what did you get that it's all about?"

She traced the largest, most ornate cross with her left hand. "That Jesus is God and was in heaven long before He was born. From forever."

"That's a good start."

"I'm still not sure I understand that whole thing."

"Would you want to?"

She cocked her head and closed her eyes. "I like things to make sense."

"But if God were completely understandable, if He made total sense to you according to human's limited knowledge, would He be a God worthy of faith and worship?"

She opened her eyes and dropped her shoulders. "I never thought of it that way."

"Faith in God is believing He is who He says He is. That belief is based on seeing the evidence He provides and trusting him with the rest. It's like having only some of the puzzle pieces and getting them to fit, yet seeing enough of the picture to get the general idea of the whole thing."

She mulled over his words. "If He is who He says He

is…."

"Yes."

"Then He's perfect, and we fall way short and are enemies of God. We…I could never measure up. No matter how hard I tried."

"That is what He says."

"But it's too simple. All I have to do is believe?" The question brought tears with its previously hidden doubts.

"Believe and repent. It's not enough to believe Jesus is Lord, you have to be willing to turn from doing things your way and follow Him."

"I'm not sure I know exactly what that means."

"You don't have to have it all figured out. You just have to be ready to submit your life to God."

One lone tear escaped and traced a trail of both regret and hope down her cheek. She forced the words past the lump in her throat. "I'm ready."

CHAPTER TWENTY-ONE

"Barrett, I've really got to go." Jen stifled a yawn. "Tomorrow's a work day."

He laughed. "Today was a work day, too. So was yesterday."

She curled her knees up and hugged the phone between her ear and shoulder. Had she really spent the last five nights on the phone with Barrett for hours on end? Yes. Ever since the day he helped her turn her life over to God. "That's why I'm so tired. How in the world can you get up for work every morning and keep me talking so late?"

"Sleep's optional. It's not like you can make it up or anything. Your body just adjusts."

"My body is not adjusting." She covered her mouth as her brain sought extra oxygen. "And if I fall asleep sitting at my desk tomorrow and get fired, it's gonna be your fault."

His howl brought a tired smile to her face. "You won't get fired. They love you."

"How do you know that?"

"I know people."

"Barrett…"

"Okay, okay. My mom's coworker's step-sister is married to the youth pastor."

"Good grief. Is there anyone you don't know?"

"I didn't know you 'til recently."

Jen's stomach somersaulted. "True."

"Anyway, the word on the street is you're a pretty hard worker."

"On the street, huh? Cliché much?"

"Better than grapevine." He broke into the song she hadn't heard in at least a decade.

She chuckled. "You're crazy."

"It's why you like me so much."

Yeah, that and your thick, curly hair, deep russet eyes, and solid biceps. How had she not laid a hand on him yet? Not even to run a finger through one bouncy curl.

A shiver ran up her spine and goose bumps raised on her arms. Home. She'd not only acquired a warm, comfortable place to live, but she now had the key to an eternal home. Why had she resisted God so long?

Oh, yeah. That whole giving up control thing. She'd have keep to working on that, but the peace that filled her since tearfully confessing everything to the Lord of all surpassed anything she could have obtained out of her own efforts.

"Jen?"

"Uh, yeah?"

"Where'd you go?"

"I fell asleep. I told you I need sleep."

"You did not."

"You're right, I didn't." She switched the phone to her left ear. How could she even begin to describe in words the joy filling her? She stifled another yawn. "Thanks for talking with me."

"Any time."

He means that. "I hope I haven't bored you to death or bugged the bejeebers out of you with all my questions."

"Of course not, Jen. I told you. If God can't be questioned, He's not worthy of faith. And when I don't know the answer, it's a good opportunity for me to dig deeper."

Her response stuck in her throat. It wasn't tears this time, but gratitude. She deserved nothing. Every time she'd made a decision only to serve herself. Every ugly word she'd spoken to her parents, even if they hadn't done much to deserve kindness.

Every time she'd snubbed her nose at God.

And still He loved her and had not only been waiting for her to return that love, but placed people in her path to reveal Himself.

"Okay, well I'm all questioned out for tonight. I really have to go. Unless you want to listen to me snore."

"I bet it's a nice snore."

Heat rushed to her cheeks. Was it wrong to want to ignore the idea of sleeping and run back to his place for a long, deep goodnight kiss? She wasn't sure, but her muscles barely had enough energy to roll onto her back, much less get out of bed. Practicality won over desire.

"You'll get to hear it and determine that for yourself in about sixty seconds."

"Okay, okay. Tomorrow then."

"Tomorrow."

She hung up and stared at the shimmering slits made by the light sneaking through the blinds.

Not only had God given her His love, but He'd also given her Barrett.

Could she trust him with her heart?

Yes. She could. A grin turned up the corners of her mouth, she murmured, "Thank you," and drifted off to sleep.

CHAPTER TWENTY-TWO

Jen glanced over her shoulder. She didn't like having to stop at the off-the-beaten path convenience store after dark, but it was the only one between Barrett's house and her place. Her and Marla's fridge had become almost completely bare, housing only a block of cheese, a few sodas, and some lettuce. Nothing even remotely breakfast like. She could make oatmeal with water, if they had any. They really needed to work out a grocery run schedule.

The cashier rang up her milk, coffee, and granola bars, giving her the total in an eastern accent. "Twenty-one, eighty-two."

She pulled the cash out of her wallet, handed it over, and waited on her change. "Thanks."

She grabbed her bag of goodies in one hand and shoved the bills and coins in her purse with the other. The bell clanged as she exited the brightly lit store and stepped out into the frigid air. The parking lot had several lights, but they couldn't have been more than forty watts each.

She fumbled for her keys, finding them at the bottom of her purse. She pulled them out and glanced back as a black sedan rolled behind her through the parking lot. The key found its mark and turned. Jen reached for the handle and gasped when a hand grabbed her arm.

"Hey, pretty thing. You shouldn't be out like this by yourself. You'll get lonely."

She looked back to see a scruffy guy in his twenties. Spiky blonde hair, unshaven, and tattoos pasted all over his arms and neck. Sneering and looking her up and down as his spindly fingers held onto her left sleeve.

She gripped her keys in her shaking hand. Her stomach lurched and she twisted her body. "Let me go."

"Nah. That doesn't sound like fun." The sneer grew and he stepped in closer, revealing a tongue ring.

The sedan pulled up behind the guy. Someone to help, maybe?

Another art covered guy leaned out the passenger window. "Come on, man, let's go."

The rear door swung open and the grubby hand yanked Jen away from her car. She screamed and whirled her hand gripping her keys at his face. She made contact and he let out a string of curse words. His grip didn't loosen, but was joined by a second hand as he shoved her towards the awaiting car. Her screams reverberated in her ears as she flailed her arms and kicked her legs. This could not be happening.

"Hey! What's going on out here?"

The guy released her and dove into the car as she fell to the ground. Tires squealed as a kind brown hand reached down and gently laid on hers.

Jen looked up into the Indian cashier's face. His brows wrinkled. "Are you okay, ma'am?"

She nodded and burst into tears, then swung her head at the sound of crunching metal. The dark, four-door car came to a rest cockeyed on the two lane road, the side smashed in by a small, red car, its front end no longer visible.

She turned back to the gentle man at her side, eyes wide. The shaking in her body seemed to relieve her of any ability to talk or think. Tears flowed freely down her face.

"I've already called 911. I left my cell in the store. Do you have one? I should probably call again to make sure they send an ambulance."

She nodded, searching the ground around her for her purse. It lay sprawled by her car.

He reached a long, thin arm and pulled it to them. She unsnapped the strap, snatched her phone out of its specially designed pocket, and handed it to him. Would her body ever stop trembling? She pulled her knees up and wrapped her arms around them, watching the scene on the road as he dialed.

Several cars had stopped near the accident. A woman, blood splattered on her face and clothes, screamed, "My baby, my baby. Someone help me."

A burly man yanked the rear passenger door several times before it opened. He moved aside. A small form hung limply against the seat belt. The mother moved in, blocking her view. Jen's heart sank.

Distant sirens grew louder and closer. The cashier still talked on her cell phone. But all the noise was drowned out by one thought. *It's all my fault.*

Cries and pleas to God filled the air.

Yes, God, where are you in this? I thought you were better than this. All good. Perfect. How could you let that little girl get hurt? I'd rather it have been me.

"Ma'am. Your phone."

She accepted the device.

"Is there someone you could call?" The soft brown eyes focused on her.

Who should she call? Marla? No, she'd already be ready for bed. Barrett? Not sure she should, Jen nodded and scrolled through to find his number. She'd added a picture to his contact information, not just…she glanced at the time…half an hour ago.

His infectious smile had no effect for the first time since she'd seen him across the church parking lot a several weeks back.

"Hey. I was wondering when I'd get my 'I got home okay' call."

"I–" She choked back a sob.

"Jen, what's wrong? Did something happen?"

"Oh, Barrett." She relayed, in choppy, broken sentences, the last few minutes of her life.

"I'll be right there."

"No, I'll be okay." Would she though? Ever?

Fire trucks, police vehicles, and two ambulances had arrived on the scene.

"Don't you even think about arguing with me. Is someone there with you?"

She nodded.

"Jen?"

"Yes," she squeaked as she watched the young child placed on a gurney, rolled, and lifted into the back of an awaiting medical emergency vehicle.

"Stay put. I'll be there in ten minutes."

"Okay." She hung up and met the cashier's raised eyebrows.

"Someone's coming to get you?"

She nodded.

A couple of officers, one male and one female, strolled towards them from the accident. The shaking which had reduced to minor tremors in her arms and legs took off again as if major, foundational plates within her were shifting and colliding.

CHAPTER TWENTY-THREE

Crying out, Jen opened her eyes. The simple warmth of Marla's den lit by the bright morning sun shining through the windows greeted her. She wasn't in the parking lot. No rough hands grabbed and jerked her. Muscular arms encircled her, though, gentle and reassuring. She looked up into Barrett's dark eyes, noting the crease in his brow.

"You okay?"

She nodded then shrugged. Tears brimmed in her eyes and blurred his face.

"You had a pretty scary night."

Barrett had a knack for understating things. The trembling began again, radiating out from her stomach to her extremities.

He smoothed her hair. "Shhh. It'll be alright. You're safe now."

"I..." She hiccupped. "I don't understand. Why would God let that happen? I put my faith in Him and had such peace. Isn't He supposed to protect me?"

He sighed. "I don't know why it happened. We may not ever have an answer. But we live in a sinful world, Jen, and God tells us in His word to be prepared for trials. He protects our hearts and our souls, but as long as we live here on earth, we'll have troubles. Just like you and I have made wrong choices that hurt others, those guys don't know the Lord and are living only for themselves. You know that way of living always hurts ourselves and other people."

She slumped in his embrace. Her neck hurt, but she didn't know whether it was from the trauma of the night before or sleeping in Barrett's arms on the sofa. He'd held her after bringing her home last night until her sobs exhausted her.

She shifted in an attempt to lessen the ache.

"So, our girl's awake." Marla strolled into the room and to the kitchenette.

"She is."

Marla pulled several items out of the fridge. "How ya feelin', Sweetie?"

Jen shrugged her shoulders again.

"I don't think she's sure yet."

"That's understandable."

Where had all the groceries come from? Another question that would most likely go unanswered.

"How about some pancakes this mornin'?" A mixing bowl came out of one of the cabinets, followed by a couple measuring cups.

"You're cooking?"

Marla laughed. "Relax, my friend. Pancakes are my specialty. Made thousands of them in my life. Unlike baked chicken and sweet potatoes."

The memory of the dry-as-the-desert meat and undercooked vegetable lifted Jen's spirits and corners of her mouth a tad. "I am a bit hungry."

"Good."

She turned, breaking out of Barrett's arms. She sat up and faced him. There was no way to stay focused while leaned into him.

"What about the little girl? I mean something happening to me, I can kinda understand that. I've made enough bad choices and deserve whatever punishment God sends my way. But that small, innocent girl, how can that be part of His plan?"

He reached out and stroked her cheek. The sparks overpowered the trembling. Had she not been so concerned, not had so many questions, she'd have thrown her arms around his neck and finally found out what it felt like to kiss him.

"First of all, God doesn't necessarily work that way. What happened to you could have been a consequence of a choice you made in the past, simply those guys' sin, or something else completely. God has a reason He lets tragedies like this filter through His hands. Sometimes we know the reason. Sometimes we don't. But that doesn't mean He's not with us or doesn't love us completely."

"I don't know, Barrett. I can't wrap my brain around this one." The picture of the unconscious child flashed in her mind.

He opened his mouth to answer, but hesitated and held a finger up. Pulling his vibrating phone from his back pocket, he answered, "Hello?"

His eyes lit up as he listened. Jen raised her eyebrows. What could he possibly be happy about?

"Yeah?"

What in the world?

"That's great, man. Thanks." He hung up and grinned at her as if he'd just won the lottery. "And sometimes He provides an answer."

"Who was that?"

"My cousin, Mark. He's an E.M.T. and I asked him to keep me updated on Natasha.

Of course Barrett would know someone who could give him information. "Natasha?"

"The little girl from the accident. Her mom said it'd be okay to pass along how she's doing."

Jen's hopes soared. She leaned forward, grabbing Barrett's hands in hers. "She's okay?"

"She's better than okay. They did an x-ray because of a suspected cracked rib. Turns out she has a heart defect no one knew about."

How was that good news? She shook her head. "I don't understand."

His grin broadened. "If she hadn't been in the accident, they may have never found it. She has a small hole in her heart, one small enough her pediatrician had never heard a heart murmur from it with a stethoscope. It would have gotten worse over time, though, and could have caused major problems for her. Without treatment or detection it could have done more damage to her body, especially her lungs. That could lead to severe weakness, physical limitations, and possibly the need for a heart and lung transplant later on and robbing her of ever having children."

Her hand flew to her mouth.

"As it is, they've already performed a simple procedure and fixed the problem. She's recovering perfectly."

"Oh, Barrett."

He captured her chin beneath his thumb and forefinger. "The accident saved that little girl's life."

CHAPTER TWENTY-FOUR

Ashley Parker embraced Jen before she could get through the doorway. "Thank you so much. I'm so sorry for what happened to you, but I'm so grateful for the accident."

It had been two weeks and Jen still had a nightmare about the attack almost every night. But as soon as she awoke and opened her eyes, God filled her with peace and joy as she recited the verses from the book of James as Barrett had sugested. 'Consider it pure joy, my brothers and sisters, whenever you face trials of many kinds, because you know that the testing of your faith produces perseverance. Perseverance must finish its work so that you will be mature and complete, not lacking anything.'

It also helped knowing those creeps were locked behind bars.

"Thank you, Mrs. Parker. And thank you for letting

me come see Natasha."

The blonde woman stepped back and clasped her hands together. "Oh, she wouldn't have it any other way. And you must be Barrett."

He stuck his hand out. "Yes, Ma'am."

"Well, come on in. Natasha's in the living room."

Jen and Barrett followed Mrs. Parker through the foyer and down a short hallway. They turned and she spotted the little girl sitting on the sofa, hair pulled back in a braid and wearing a delicate pink dress. She smiled to match the pint size greeting.

"Miss Jennifer!" Natasha hopped up and ran to Jen, throwing her arms around her legs.

"Hi, Natasha. I'm glad to see you're feeling much better."

The six-year-old stepped back, looking up with bright blue eyes identical to her mother's. "Did you hear? I had a hole in my heart. The doctors found it because of the crash and now I'm all better."

"Yes, Natasha, I heard all about it. I'm so happy for you."

"I made you something." She bounded across the room and grabbed a sheet of paper off a coffee table, returning and handing it to Jen.

The budding artist had drawn a picture of two cars crashed, a little girl with a large heart with a hole, three doctors surrounding her, and an angel hovering above them all. She pointed to the floating figure. "See that? That's you, Miss Jennifer. You're my angel God sent to save my life."

Tears filled Jen's eyes. God had used her. Her, despite her sin and lack of faith until recently. He'd put her in the right place at the right time, and even though the night had been traumatic, she hadn't really been hurt.

"I think you're the angel, Natasha. Thank you for reminding me of God's great love."

~*~

Three hours later, with a full stomach and cheeks sore from smiling, Jen held Barrett's hand as they walked out of the Parker's home to his car.

"That's one special little girl."

"Yes, she is." He leaned against the passenger door instead of opening it for her. "And I think you have a friend for life."

"I certainly hope so."

"Me, too." Barrett stepped closer and held her gaze.

"Are we still talking about me and Natasha?"

"Well, in a way."

Jen raised her eyebrows.

"If she's going to be your little companion for a lifetime, then I guess she'll be mine, too."

Jen searched his face. What was he saying?

He reached into his pocket and lifted a fisted hand between them. "And I think Natasha would make a great flower girl."

Her heart sped up, as if jolted by surge of electricity. "A flower girl?"

"Yes, at our wedding. If you'll have me." Barrett opened his hand, revealing a diamond encircled sapphire ring.

Her mouth flew open.

"Jen, I love you. I love the way you challenge me. I love your honesty. I love your vulnerability. I know this has been quick, we've only known each other a short time, but I feel I've known you forever. And I want to spend the rest of my forever getting to know you more. Will you marry me?"

Was this really happening? Was Barrett, whom she hadn't known three months ago, proposing marriage? Had he lost his mind? Had she? Because everything in her screamed, 'Yes!'

Could she trust him with her heart? She looked into his dark eyes. They had talked more over the last five or six weeks than she and Ian had talked in almost as many years.

She knew him better. She hadn't pushed this. Hadn't

seen it coming. But it felt perfect.

God's peace filled her and the answer to her questions and Barrett's came out in one fragile, breathless word: "Yes."

He clasped her left hand and slid the ring onto her fourth finger. He then leaned down and brushed his lips against hers in the lightest, most euphoric promise of more. So much more.

Epilogue

Jen wrapped her arms around Barrett as he twirled her around the dance floor. Her off-white gown with tiny blue flowers matching her sapphire engagement ring speckled across the elegant material swirled and her smile grew even wider. 'Redeemed,' a new song to her, played as she danced her first dance with her husband.

The small ballroom was filled with friends and family. Mostly Barrett's. She had sent her parents an invitation, but hadn't received a response. At least Aunt Bobbie had been able to attend.

She leaned her head on Barrett's shoulder and closed her eyes, soaking in the words. She could relate to every one. Once she'd believed what she'd been told her whole life: she was worthless. Now she grasped the truth that she'd been redeemed and set free by God's love. She was a new person and had a new life. She'd spend the rest of it learning about Jesus and who said she was in him. And loving Barrett.

She looked up and planted one more kiss on her

husband's lips. He pulled her closer and staked his claim. The song ended and she reluctantly pulled away.

Another song began as Barrett swept his mother across the floor. Jen swooped up Natasha in her arms. "You look beautiful, Natasha. Your dress matches your blue eyes perfectly."

"And your ring." The little girl giggled as she ogled the stone now adorned with a gold and diamond band slid beneath it. She reached up and placed her chubby hand on Jen's cheek. "I'm glad God brought us together, Miss Jennifer."

Jen squeezed the girl in a one-arm hug. "Me, too."

They swayed to the music until it ended. She set Natasha down. "I have to go out again, but save a dance for me."

Natasha beamed. "I will."

If Jen got any happier, she'd pass out in that very spot. She'd always worried about the father-daughter dance, but God had taken care of that, too. When the wedding loomed only a week away and she hadn't gotten a response from her parents, Barrett's dad asked if he could dance with her at their reception.

She now accepted his hand and followed him onto the dance floor, her cheeks aching from her overflowing joy.

Her Whole Self

Thank you, Father, for everything. A job, a home, a family, and most of all for Your perfect love.

Dear Reader,

I am so honored and blessed that you have chosen to read **Her Whole Self**. *It is a story meant to show that while we often look to things of this world to satisfy us, there is only one way to be completely fulfilled: through the indwelling of the Holy Spirit, put in us when we step into a faith relationship with God through His Son Jesus, the promised Messiah. It is only through His love and the love He's provided through His other children I've learned to see myself through His eyes: a daughter of the King of kings and Lord of lords, a precious, cherished child, and a redeemed sinner who can truly live a fulfilled, successful life in Him.*

As you saw with Jen, and have most likely experienced yourself, faithfully walking with Christ does not protect us from pain, suffering, grief, or heartache. As long as we live on this planet, those things will be a part of our lives. However, God's promises will hold us through each one of the challenges we face so that we can eventually rejoice in everything, including trials. We can do this if and only when we place our complete trust in the fact that He loves us more than we can imagine. I hope you know this extravagant love.

It is as simple and as hard as turning your life completely over to God and submitting yourself to Him daily. It's about entering into that relationship with God through believing He is who He says He is and drawing closer to Him for the rest of your life. It goes against almost everything our society and culture tells us is important, but has rewards beyond what is humanly possible to understand.

My hope is that if you haven't stepped into that relationship yet, that you will. And if you have given Jesus your heart, yet still hold back part of yourself from him, that you will prayerfully give Him Your Whole Self.

By His grace,
Tracy Wainwright
www.tracywainwright.com

Other Books by Tracy Wainwright

Nonfiction

Treasures of Healthy Living
Teacher's Manual

Living Praise: a journal of thanks-living

Children's Books

Counting from Creation
Apple vs. Asparagus

Find out more about the author and
her books at:
www.tracywainwright.com

Marla smiled at the groom twirling his bride across the floor. She had grown to love Jen so dearly over the last few months. Watching her come to know Christ and grow in him.

The song ended and a new one began. A perfect metaphor for where she was at the moment. Her and Jen's new friendship would change now. There wouldn't be any more late night gabbing or last minute trips to the movies. Once again, Marla would go home to an empty apartment every night.

An arm draped over her shoulders and she jumped. She looked up at Carlos' grinning face. "You could give a girl a heart attack, sneaking up on her like that."

"I didn't sneak, you were a million miles away."

It was true. She had been. Missing Jen already. And now she needed to put some space between herself and Carlos. The flopping he caused in her stomach was too dangerous. She shrugged out of his arm and took a step back.

"Oh, just happy for Barrett and Jen." She returned her gaze to the couple, now dancing with a group of friends. Jen's head reared back as she laughed at something her new husband had whispered in her ear. "She's radiant."

"She is." Carlos stepped closer. "And so are you."

Heat rushed to Marla's cheeks. No. She couldn't fall for him. Okay, she couldn't keep falling for him. The feelings she'd began having towards him didn't matter. They weren't realistic. Marriage and kids and all those dreams had died long ago for her. She refused to take the risk. Scanning the room for an escape, she spotted Cara next to the cake table chatting with the pastor's daughter.

"Thanks, Carlos. I hate to run, but I really need to talk to Cara about some missions stuff. I'll catch you later."

Marla wove her way through the celebrators to safety, refusing to look back and see if Carlos had moved on or planted a puppy dog, hurt face on. She didn't care. She couldn't afford to care.

~*~

While passionate about God, serving him, and leading others to him, Marla has hidden deep cracks in her inner being. She says she trusts God with everything, but there are some questions she'd like answers to. Seeing Jen's faith burst forth and flourish combined with once again living by herself and with her old thoughts, Marla faces a difficult question. Can she trust God completely with her future when the past has predicted more pain?

~*~

I invite you to join me for Marla's adventure: *Her Broken Places*. Installments will be released monthly in RENEW Magazine, distributed in Hampton Roads, VA. You can find digital issues @www.renewvamagazine.com.

The complete story and novella is scheduled to be released in October 2015.

Made in the USA
San Bernardino, CA
26 February 2014